The Good Deacon

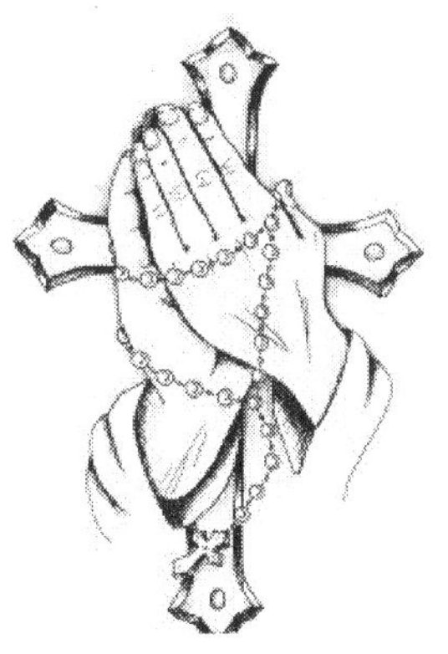

Written By

Autumn Crum

Copyright

Printed in the USA

Publisher: Crum Publishing, LLC

Graphic Designer: Fiverr

Editor: Goal Digger Literary Services

ISBN: 9781658178266

This book is for my readers. Without you there is no me… Let's connect!

Prologue

Warm air blasted through the vents as Earl and Margaret Robinson navigated their old station wagon through the icy roads of Conners, Georgia. Margaret's heart was racing. She hadn't heard from their daughter Teresa since Thursday and today was Monday. Maybe it was mother's intuition, but something wasn't right. Teresa never missed a day without phoning her mother. They talked on the telephone sometimes three times a day. The factory where Teresa worked said she hadn't come by to pick up her paycheck on Friday and when she missed Sunday dinner Earl and Margaret both began to panic. She never missed a Sunday dinner; at least not since she had come home from rehab.

The Robinson family struggled for many years through Teresa's drug addiction. It had started out as a small weed habit developing in her freshman year of high school and had morphed into a full-fledged crack cocaine addiction by the time Teresa was an adult. But after countless prayers and a court ordered rehab the Robinsons were proud to say that their daughter had gotten on her feet and completely turned her life around. She stopped hanging with her old friends, got herself a job, and started attending church. Teresa had also started the process of getting her GED and had even managed to scrape together enough money to rent a place near her job in Conners. But now she was missing.

The feeling of impending doom hit Margaret sometime in the middle of the night. It was an incredibly suffocating emotion that crept up her spine and wouldn't allow her to breathe let alone rest. She told her husband she had to know where their baby girl was, and she had to know now. Could Teresa have fallen back into her old ways? Could something worse have happened to her? Earl tried to calm Margaret, but she was still on pins and needles the entire 45-minute ride from Mayville to Conners.

Gravel crunched under the tires as the Robinsons finally pulled up the driveway of their destination. The sun had yet to peak but the orange glow offered a peaceful backdrop against the pale-yellow exterior of the double wide trailer where Teresa lived. A thin veil of freshly fallen snow lay like a blanket across Teresa's yard. Earl killed the engine before he and Margaret got out. Margaret's worried brown eyes surveyed her surroundings. A wind chime clanked against the steal gutter as the wind blew but other than that the air was dead quiet. She followed nervously behind her husband; making their way to the front door. Earl's face displayed concerned when he realized the front door was slightly ajar.

"Wait here" he told Margaret.

Margaret watched frantically as her husband pulled his pistol from its holster and entered the mobile home with caution. Not wanting to be left alone on the cold desolate porch, Margaret entered the mobile home as well.

Gospel music could be heard coming from the master bedroom. "Teresa!" Earl called out "Reese Cup you home?" The inside of Teresa's trailer was freezing cold but beads of sweat still dripped from Earls forehead as he inched down the hallway; unsure of what awaited him. Midway down the hallway something squished under his feet. It was water. The entire carpet in the hallway and bedroom was saturated with it. As he got closer the song became clearer.

It was "Oh Happy Day" by Edwin Hawkins; one of Teresa's favorite songs. She learned it in the church choir when she was a little girl and had been singing it ever since. Matter of fact she sung it every time it came on. So why wasn't she singing along to the captivating lyrics now? Earl got his answer when he pushed open the door to the bathroom that was connected to the master bedroom.

"Oh my god! Teresa!" Earl's screams jolted Margaret upright. She ran to his aid but quickly regretted it. Her beloved daughter lay naked; floating face down in the tub. Water still trickled from the faucet. Margaret let out an earth-shattering scream; the type of scream only a mother can make when witnessing her daughter's lifeless body floating in a watery grave.

"He killed her!" was all Margaret managed to say before the room started spinning and everything went dark.

One

Six Months Later...

*B*utt naked and bent over a granite countertop. That is how 35-year-old Piper Jackson found out her husband was being unfaithful. The sight of her husband's hairy ass being rammed by another man would forever be burned into her memory. Ten years she was married to Leland Jackson and never knew he was a homosexual. Sure, there were signs. The fact that their sex life had been pretty much nonexistent after the birth of their second child may have been a cause for concern for most women, but Piper just assumed their marriage had just fizzled out. She tried to rekindle the romance by buying lingerie and scheduling romantic getaways. Leland would act like he was all into it but deep down inside she knew he wasn't. Piper was putting in all the effort to please her man, but it turned out that no matter how good she rode his pole she could never screw her husband better than another man could.

The pain of Leland's betrayal rocked Piper to her core but what he did next would shatter her world forever. Four months after they separated Leland died unexpectedly of a heart attack. Not only had the bastard betrayed Piper, but he left their kids fatherless, and the icing on the cake… He left a will behind naming his lover "Mateo Valdes" as the sole beneficiary of his estate. Broke and penniless Piper had no choice but to load up a U-haul truck, gather her kids, and head back home to Conners, Georgia.

"Mama are we there yet?" Piper's nine-year-old son Leland Jr. asked. She peered over at his handsome brown face. L.J was small for his age; very scrawny with a big head like his father.

"Almost" Piper replied, struggling to put a smile on her face.

"Good, because I sure am hungry." Piper's six-year-old daughter Phoebe chimed in, rubbing her rotund belly.

"I hear ya' Phoebe May." Piper replied. "I promise as soon as we make it off this highway, we will find you something to eat."

"I hope it's McDonalds!" Phoebe said twisting her lips.

Piper shook her head at Phoebe's sassiness as she made the exit off highway 80. Conners, Georgia. Population 752; a teeny tiny town nestled between Albany and Atlanta. Conners was known for its railroads and nothing else. It was the place where Piper grew up, and the place she had promised herself never to return. But here she was, a newly widowed single mother going back to the quiet laziness of small-town living.

"Oh, look there's a Barbecue truck. Who wants Barbecue?"

"Ooh I do! I do!" L.J. piped up.

"Not me" Phoebe snapped giving too much attitude. "I want McDonalds not no burnt meat!"

"Sorry Phoebe May you've been out voted." Piper replied, "We're having Bar-B-Que tonight."

***

Conners, Georgia was where Charles Brewer called home. He loved it there. After over thirty two years in the military he and his wife Ruby had settled into Conners so he could start his job on the railroad as a mechanic. He finally retired at the ripe old age of 65 and decided he would pursue his ultimate dream and that was becoming a grill master. He took a leap of faith and some of the money from his savings and bought himself a food truck. Charlie's BBQ was hands down the best damn Barbecue stand this side of the Mississippi River. People came from miles around to taste Charlie's BBQ made with his secret sauce he called "The South in Yo' Mouth".

"Mmm mmmm Mr. Charlie I swear you never disappoint." His best customer Deputy Yance Williams was singing Charlie's praises as he smacked on a rib tip.

"Deputy Williams you are up here almost every day eating my ribs. Be careful or your gut gone stick out further than mine" Mr Charlie grinned, displaying his one gold tooth.

"I know man!" Deputy Williams replied with his mouth full of meat. "But this is the only way a brother can get a home cooked meal."

"You need you a woman. I keep telling you that!" Charlie chastised handing Deputy Williams a napkin.

"Where am I gonna get her from?" Deputy Williams griped. "Every woman around these parts is either married or too old to care. I'm telling you unless God himself drops a woman out of the sky I'm destined to be a bachelor eating up your ribs for the rest of my life."

They both shared a good hearty laugh. Out of the corner of his eyes Charlie spotted a U-haul truck with a grey Mercedes SUV hitched to the back of it coming from the direction of the interstate. His heart swelled a bit when the moving truck pulled into the gas station parking lot where his food truck was parked. He knew that whoever was inside that truck wouldn't be able to resist the smell of his delicious BBQ wafting up through the smokers. He was surprised to see such a small young woman climb out of a truck so big.

"Stop running!" she called after two small children who had scurried out of the truck behind her.

Deputy Williams paused mid chew as he and Mr. Charlie both stared at the lovely woman. Deputy William's eyes suddenly lit up with excitement when he realized he knew her.

"Piper? Piper is that you?"

The woman who seemed to be caught up in her own thoughts looked at Deputy Williams and squinted her eyes

"Yance Williams?"

"Yes, it's me!" He smiled a Kool aid smile.

"Oh, my goodness, Yance!" Piper went in for a hug then stood back to get a good look at him. Yance Williams was the high school sweetheart who had broken Piper's heart when he accepted a full ride scholarship to LSU and left her behind in Conners. "Boy, look at you. You haven't changed a bit since ninth grade. I thought you would've been playing pro football by now. What you doing back in Conners?"

"Old knee injury set your boy down." Deputy Williams admitted. "Plus, I'm an ol' country boy at heart you know that."

"Yeah you always were." Piper smiled.

"Hi there Mister." Phoebe's small voice

greeted; hands still clinging to her mother's skirt.

"Well hi there pretty girl!" Deputy Williams bent down smiling at the little girl. "What's your name?"

"I'm Phoebe May." Phoebe replied with sass. "Who are you?"

"I'm Deputy Williams."

"Deputy Williams why were you looking at my mama like that? You like her or something?"

"Oh my goodness, ignore her please." Piper blushed with embarrassment. "This is my son Leland Jr."

Deputy Williams stood upright and looked down at L.J. "Whats up lil man?"

He extended his fist for a bump to which LJ reluctantly bumped before looking up at his mother.

"Mama can we eat now?"

"Hush boy I told you I would feed you!" Piper chastised "Don't be rude."

"Oh if you're hungry then you've come to the right place L.J. because Mr. Charlie here has barbecue so good it will make you wanna slap your mama!" Deputy Williams said erupting in laughter.

"Slap my mama?" LJ looked confused.

"Boy I wish you would even try it." Piper laughed; her doe brown eyes landed on Charlie. "Hey there Mr. Charlie how are you today?"

Charlie was so busy staring at Piper's beautiful dimpled smile he hadn't even realize she was speaking to him. "Huh? Oh hey. Hey, Darling how are you doing?"

"Mr. Charlie you remember Piper don't you?" Deputy Williams inquired. "She used to be in Ms. Ruby's Bible study class back in the day."

"Vaguely" Charlie shook his head, his eyes glazed over as he eyed the young beauty intently behind his glasses. He couldn't place her face but she did look familiar to him. "Who your people?"

"The Crosby's down in Winder Gate. Ain't but a handful of us, tho'. Pearl is my mother."

"Oh sista Crosby!" Charlie beamed. "Yes ma'am I know your mama very well. She was one of the first people Ruby and I met when we moved to Conners. Nice lady. See her every Sunday morning at church. I never remember her having a daughter, tho'. Especially not one as pretty as you."

"Oh stop it! Flattery gets you everywhere Mr. Charlie." Piper blushed. "How is Miss Ruby?"

"Who?"

"Your wife…You two are still married right?"

Charlie hesitated then admitted. "Yeah…Yes… mmm hmm." He nodded. "She's fine…Ruby's doing just fine."

"That's good." Piper nodded.

"Mama!" The kids whined. "We hungry!"

"Oh yeah, Mr. Charlie please tell me you can whip up something quick for us." Piper pleaded. "I got two starving kids here."

"Yes ma'am Miss Piper I gotcha covered. Be right back." Charlie disappeared to fix their food.

"Ol' Piper Crosby!" Deputy Williams settled into a soft smile as he peered at Piper. "What finally brings you to town? Coming to check on your mama?"

"More like coming to live with my mama." Piper said sadly. "And it's Jackson now. I was married and now I'm not."

"Oh I didn't know-"

"It's fine." Piper shook her head.

"I didn't mean to pry. I'm sorry."

"Don't be." Piper brushed him off. "I mean it sucks having to start my life over at 35 but at least I got my two beautiful kids, a place to lay our heads, and my sanity."

"I heard that" Deputy Williams agreed. "Plus starting over doesn't have to suck ya' know. Life is like a book. One chapter closes and another one opens. All you gotta do is turn the page."

The look in the deputy's eyes gave Piper pause. The old ember in them that was threatening to catch fire was quickly extinguished when three Styrofoam containers wrapped in plastic was suddenly plopped down in front of them.

"Order up!" Charlie announced shoving the food in between them. "Now Miss Piper I tried a different rub on the ribs this time. They got a little kick to 'em but not much. I put some chicken in here just in case they're too spicy. There's some extra corn fritters in there for the kids. I also gave you a slice of my lemon cake and one for your mama too."

"Thank you so much, Mr. Charlie I really appreciate this. What's my total?" Piper asked opening up her wallet.

"No Charge. This is on the house." He beamed proudly.

Piper's eyes bulged as she looked at Deputy Williams. "Mr. Charlie this is a lot of food. You sure?"

"Positive!"

"Because I can pay for this."

"I insist." Charlie rejected her debit card. "Let me be the first to say, welcome home."

His smile was sincere and it warmed Piper's heart. "Well thank you Mr. Charlie."

"You're welcome Darling. Tell your mama I said hey."

"Will do." Piper nodded swinging her eyes to Yance. "See you around Deputy Williams."

"I can guarantee you that." Deputy Williams watched Piper's backside as she walked back to the truck behind her children. "Umph, umph, umph that woman is still fine."

"Yeah…" Charlie agreed hypnotized. "She is something to look at."

"Welp." Deputy Williams picked up his Stetson and placed it over his head. "I guess I better get going."

"Where you going?" Charlie snarled.

"Back to work."

"Not until you give me my ten dollars for that rib sandwich you just ate!"

“Mr. Charlie you just let that woman walk away with half a hog and you gone sweat me for ten little dollars?”

“Well if them dollars that little you won't miss them now pay up.” Charlie held out his hand until Deputy Williams finally slapped a ten dollar bill in it.

“Thank you kindly! Enjoy the rest of your day Deputy.” Charlie smiled.

“You cold blooded Mr. Charlie.” Deputy Williams shook his head laughing as he walked away.

“You have no idea son.” Charlie mumbled under his breath as he watched the U-haul truck disappear out of sight. The smile faded from his face. “You have no idea.”

Two

"Oh my goodness are those my grand babies all grown up!" Pearl Crosby greeted her daughter and grandchildren in the yard as the U-haul pulled up. Pearl was a kindly looking woman with rich cinnamon brown skin that never aged.

"Hey grandma!" LJ greeted. He and Phoebe were out the door and in their grandmothers arms before the truck could stop good.

"Bout time y'all got here." Pearl fussed looking up at Piper. "What took you so long?"

Piper let out a sigh.

"Hey Mama!" she droned and hugged her mother.

"Well ain't you a sight for sore eyes." Pearl hugged her daughter back. "Um well… you look good."

"You don't need to lie to me Mama." Piper smiled weakly. "I already know I look a hot mess. I sure do feel like it anyway."

"Well you're home now baby girl." Pearl gave a warm pat on Piper's back then turned towards the house. "Y'all come on in and I'll cook you a good meal."

"Oh no Mama don't worry about it. Me and the kids stopped to a barbecue spot right off the highway." Pearl stopped in her tracks and looked at Piper with a peculiar look on her face.

"You talkin about Charlie's BBQ spot?"

"Yes."

"What did he say to you?"

"Nothing really… Just wanted me to tell you hello."

"Hmm" was all Pearl said.

"What does that mean?" Piper queried.

Pearl shook her head. “Oh it’s nothing.” She quickly masked the uncomfortable look on her face with a smile “It’s just… oh nothing I’ll tell you later. I’m sure you guys are tired. Come on in and get comfortable.”

The Crosby home hadn’t changed much since Piper was a teenager. The same old nauseating country apple décor was in the kitchen, plastic still covered every surface in the living room. Even Pipers bedroom still looked like Word Up magazine had thrown up all over the walls.

Piper plopped down on the bed and stared up at the ceiling. As she watched the collection of dust spin around on the ceiling fan, thoughts were swirling around in her head a mile a minute. She had to get a job, find a place to rent, get the kids in school and start her life over. And she had to do it all by herself.

“Stop! I’ma tell mama.”

“I don’t care! Tell mama!”

“Mamaaaaaaa!”

“Ugh fuck my life!” Piper moaned into the pillow. So much for getting a nap in. Piper made her way back to the dining room where Pearl was playing referee with the kids.

"You two sit down and shut up… now!"

LJ and Phoebe reluctantly took their seats at the dining table where Pearl had plates set down in front of them.
Piper slid down in a chair and asked, "What are y'all in here fighting about anyway?"

"Phoebe told grandma you had a new boyfriend." LJ said laughing.

"Huh?"

"She does have a new boyfriend!" Phoebe quipped.

"Does not!"

"Does too!"

"Does-"

"Enough!" Piper said, "Phoebe what in the world are you talking about?"

"That nice policeman was giving you the googley eyes mama." Phoebe answered tearing into a piece of chicken. "I think he likes you."

“Who is she talking about?” Pearl asked confused.

“Oh just Yance Williams.” Piper waved dismissively. “We saw him earlier at Mr Charlie’s barbecue stand.”

“Yance Williams!” Pearl lit up with excitement. “I think you may be on to something there Phoebe May. That boy is a fine young man. God fearing and single too might I add. Your father used to always tell you, Yance should’ve been your husband instead of Leland.”

“Well God Rest daddy’s soul. I wished I had listened to him. Then maybe I wouldn’t be in this mess I’m in.” Piper sighed.

“It’s going to be okay baby don’t you worry; God makes no mistakes. He'll bring you through it.” Pearl assured. “You’re home now. Home is the best place to be.”

Three

Tired and sweaty, Charlie pulled his 1984 pickup truck hauling his grill onto the dust covered road that led to his property. Ten whole acres of God's green earth and it all belonged to him. He quickly filled his farm with cows, pigs, chickens, and even a couple of goats. Fruit trees also lined the back portion of the property which consisted of peaches, navel oranges, and granny smith apples.

"Charlie is that you? Bout time you get here!" Ruby's aggravating voice grated on Charlie's last nerve soon as his foot hit the rickety wooden porch. The woman's funk hit his large nostrils as soon as he opened up the screen door.

"Charlie!" Ruby screamed again.

"I'm here Ruby." Charlie mumbled as he waddled his tired body into the living room.

Nearly 600lbs of a woman that had completely given up on herself greeted him with a look of contempt on her face. Ruby used to be such a beautiful and fit woman when Charlie first met her back in 1969. He hardly recognized the brown hippopotamus in the moo-moo gown busting the springs on the recliner. She sat in the same place he had left her that morning watching Steve Harvey's Family Feud on the new widescreen television that sat on top of the broke down floor model television.

"Bout time you got here negro!" Ruby fussed in between breaths. "Had me in this place all day after I messed myself. Had to call Johnnie Mae over to help clean me up. Why didn't you answer your phone Charles?"

"I didn't hear it ring."

"Stop lying Charlie!" Ruby screamed; her giant arms flapping all over the place. "That's all you do is lie. Swear you good for nothing. I should've listened to my daddy when he told me not to marry your sorry ass."

"I wish you would've listened to him too!" Charlie mumbled.

"What you say?"

"Nothing Ruby." Charlie quickly corrected; standing in place while his wife continued to berate him.

Once Ruby had successfully chewed Charlie out, she squinted her eyes into slits and glared at him like he was her enemy. "Did you at least bring me something to eat?" Ruby snapped. "Did you at least do that? Huh?"

"Yes Ruby I bought you something to eat."

Her eyes bulged. "Well don't just stand there nigga get me the damn food!"

Charlie rushed to hand her the Styrofoam plate he had set aside for her. Without hesitation Ruby ripped the top of the container and tore into a rib like a hungry gorilla. Her double chin vibrated as she hummed her satisfaction. Charlie tried his best to hide his disgust while he watched her stuff her face with mac 'n cheese, potato salad, collard greens, and bake beans. He was disappointed by the way Ruby had just let herself go over the years.

About ten years into their 49 years of marriage a doctor sat the both of them down and told Ruby point blank that she might as well have been born a man because she would never be able to conceive a child nor carry a child to term. Charlie believed Ruby gave up after that. She was hurting so she ate… and ate... and ate. Now she was big, miserable, and making his life a living hell. *Fat Funky Bitch!*

Charlie couldn't stand to watch Ruby killing herself with food any longer, so he retreated to the bedroom to get out of his soot and greased stained clothes. As the steam from the shower filled the bathroom Charlie caught a glimpse of himself in the mirror. He wasn't a bad looking man, yet age was quickly catching up to Charlie. His vision was blurry at best with glasses and Ole Arthritis had settled into his hips and knees. He had worked hard to build the life he did, but something wasn't quite right. Something was missing in his life.

That's when he thought about Piper. He couldn't imagine what knucklehead had done her wrong and left her a single mother. She was young and beautiful. He was sure she was probably fertile enough to give him an heir and that's just what he needed; a family to make him feel alive again. A creepy smile inched onto Charlie's face.

"Piper Brewer… I like the sound of that."

Four

Praise God, from whom all blessings flow;
Praise Him, all creatures here below;
Praise Him above, ye heavenly host;
Praise Father, Son, and Holy Ghost!

The choir of Mount Olive Missionary Baptist Church sang the doxology off key as the congregation joined in. It was hot inside the sanctuary and the fans were already being passed out as guests were starting to sit for worship service. Charlie Brewer sat in his deacon seat with his mind wandering. Wearing the poop brown suit that Ruby had picked after she reminded him to once again put her on the sick-and-shut-in list for praying. Charlie was embarrassed to have to ask the congregation for that considering Ruby's only sickness was that her fat ass couldn't make it off the couch and that was the reason why she was shut in. *Fat! Funky! BITCH!*

As Charlie thought of ways to rid himself of his headache the doors to the sanctuary opened and Charlie felt his heart flutter inside his chest. There she was, looking like one of those models from a JC Penny magazine. Charlie watched in amazement as

Piper entered the sanctuary wearing a pretty sundress with large yellow flowers clinging to her voluptuous body. She had on a white wide brim hat that accentuated her rosy cheekbones. He couldn't help but stare at her supple cleavage poking through the top part of the dress.

He watched anxiously as Piper and her mother ushered her kids into the sanctuary. She sat down and removed her hat then took in a breath as her almond shaped eyes scanned the pulpit. She caught Charlie staring at her as he sat next to the pastor. She smiled at him and he could've sworn she winked at him too. He parted his lips in a crooked smile back to her. Charlie couldn't wait for the service to be over with. As soon as the benediction was given, he made a mad dash to where Piper was.

"Hi, Miss Piper" he smiled nervously.

She was fussing with her kids when she finally looked up and noticed him. "Hey there Mr. Charlie. How are you?"

Her scent was intoxicating as she leaned in and offered him a side hug. "I'm good Darling… Are you hungry? We have some good ol' fried chicken being served in the fellowship hall. You should come."

"Oh, wow that sounds great..."

"Did somebody say fried chicken?" Charlie's lip involuntarily curled in annoyance as Deputy Williams approached them and inserted himself between Charlie and Piper.

"Hello Piper… Mrs. Crosby, you're looking amazing as usual." Deputy Williams hugged them both and offered Pearl a peck on the cheek.

"Oh stop it." Pearl blushed. "And what have I told you about calling me Mrs. Crosby?"

"I'm sorry is Sister Pearl better?"

"Mom sounds even better." Pearl replied with a sly smile

"Mama…" Piper interjected.

"Just kidding." Pearl cut her eyes sideways at Charlie briefly before returning her smile to Deputy Williams. "Alright y'all let's get ourselves down to this fellowship hall before Johnnie May eat up all the chicken."

As they walked away from Charlie leaving him stewing in the sanctuary his undeniable desire for Piper began to stir in his gut.

"Mr. Charlie are you coming?" Piper called back over her shoulder. The way she was smiling at him made his heart skip a beat. He was sure she would be his forever come hell or high water.

Five

"*O*oh Mama can I have these?" L.J was excited as he held up a box of fruit snacks.

"Yeah how much are they?"

"4.99"

"4.99?" Piper shrieked. "Five dollars just because the box has Spider Man across the front. No sir I don't think so. Put that back."

"What about the princess fruit snacks?" Phoebe inquired.

"Those are the same price Phoebe. The answer is still no. I keep telling you two Mama doesn't have a whole lot of money to spend right now."

"No fair" L.J. pouted.

"Daddy would've let us have them." Phoebe retorted.

"Well your *Daddy* is not here is he?" Piper immediately felt a tinge of guilt as the words slipped from her lips. Luckily her cellphone chimed distracting her momentarily. “Hello?”

“Good morning Mrs. Jackson. Lee Brown here of Lee Brown and Associates."

“Lee!” Piper sighed with relief at the sound of her lawyer’s voice. “I’ve been waiting on your call for two weeks now. Please tell me you got some good news for me.”

“Well” Lee hesitated. “Not quite.”

“Not quite? What does that mean?”

“Before you fly off the handle let me explain.” Lee interjected. “We filed the motion to contest the will. But of course, Valdez is fighting the claim... which we anticipated. What we were NOT anticipating is Valdez coming forth with a child he claims he and Leland were in the process of adopting before Leland’s untimely death.”

“What... in... the... hell are you saying to me right now?” Piper gritted. “There’s a child involved?”

“Indeed, there is Mrs. Jackson, and if Leland’s name is on any of those adoption papers then that child is entitled to a portion of his estate. All of his assets would then have to go through probate.”

“Well how long does that take?” She asked in fustration.

“Best case scenario a month... worse case a year.”

“A year?!” Piper shouted so loud she startled the store clerk that was stocking the shelves. She mouthed the word “sorry” before whispering harshly. “I can’t even afford to buy my two children their own box of fruit snacks. What the hell am I going to do for a year Lee?”

“Uh have you thought about maybe getting a job?” Lee asked nervously.

“Of course I have but that’s not exactly easy considering I live in the middle of Mayberry now and I have no work experience. It’s not like anyone’s knocking down my door offering me a job.” Piper rolled her eyes. “Anyway, let’s change the subject. What’s going on with my property?”

"I have a few interested prospects. There should be an offer made soon. I am working non-stop to release some of your stress." Lee assured Piper.

Piper ended the call with her attorney feeling defeated. All the years she had loved, catered, and invested in her husband and he wrote her off like a bad check.

Six

"Get the chunky peanut butter not the smooth. And I want a gallon of pralines and cream ice cream; Blue Bell brand not that cheap generic mess you always get me. It's a shame I gotta explain all this to you but you just too stupid to figure it out by yourself Charles!" Ruby griped over the phone as Charlie pulled his truck into the parking lot of the Shop-N-Save.

"I got it Ruby." Charlie droned rolling his eyes. "I promise to get everything on this list you gave me and I will get it right. Okay?"

"You had better! And hurry up too. Don't be out there lollygagging with my food ya hear me?"

"The sooner you stop nagging me, the sooner I can go in this store and pick up these groceries!" Charlie snapped as the phone line went dead. *Fat Funky Bitch!*
Charlie tossed his cellphone on the seat and allowed his eyes to adjust to the blazing sun as he scanned the parking lot in search of a parking space near the

entrance.

Sitting right in front he spotted Piper's SUV parked in the space near a concrete medium. Charlie smiled as he quickly whipped into the adjacent parking space. For a moment he had to wrestle with his urges but in the end his urges won. He pulled a pocket knife from his glove compartment, walked over to Piper's car and slit the front tire. A breath of satisfaction rushed from his lungs as he heard the tire flatten. Charlie folded up the knife and slid it in his pocket. Then he casually walked into the store whistling. *"Oh Happy Day."*

"Hey Mr. Charlie" one of the female cashiers spoke to him.

"Hey there Darling how you doing?" Charlie replied reaching for a basket.

"Good!" She answered giddily her sandy blonde hair pulled up in a sassy ponytail. "We got some greens in. Fresh from my daddy's farm."

Charlie smiled at the young woman behind his prescription eyeglasses. "Is that so?"

"Yes sir."

"I'll have to check that out." Charlie said as he placed a toothpick in his mouth and wandered the store.

His mind was now consumed with thoughts of Piper as he searched for her throughout the supermarket. Finally Charlie spotted her at the deli arguing with somebody on the phone. She seemed to be frustrated about something. This was perfect timing for him.

"Next time you call me you had better have good news!" she fussed into the phone before hanging it up and throwing it in her purse.

He watched Piper intently as she ordered a pound of turkey meat from the lady behind the counter. The little boy who was eating on his free cookie spotted Charlie first.

"Hi Mr. Charlie!" He greeted the old man running up for a hug.

Charlie tried not to cringe as L.J. rubbed his chocolate chip crumbed hands all over his white pants. Piper spun around and her supple red painted lips twisted into a warm smile.

"Hey there Mr. Charlie." She hugged him while he inhaled her scent and hoped she hadn't taken notice of him doing that.

"What y'all got going on here?" Charlie asked

watching Phoebe's short legs dangle from the buggy.

"Oh nothing just doing some light shopping; you?"

"Same." Charlie stood awkwardly eyeing Piper until she finally spoke.

"Well... um... see you around?"

"Oh yes ma'am." Charlie quickly moved out of Piper's way. "See ya' soon."
He waved at the children and watched them disappear around the corner. As soon as they were out of sight, Charlie took off like a bat out of hell to the other side of the store scrambling to get whatever Ruby had on that list. At this point he didn't give a damn if he got the Blue Bell ice cream or if the peanut butter had a crunch to it or not. He had to get to Piper and his timing had to be perfect.

***

You have got to be freaking kidding me! "Piper spat. "These tires are brand new!" Seeing that her tire was flat she whipped out her cell phone to call roadside assistance.

"Hello and thank you for calling Triple A. Are you in need of roadside assistance?" A friendly voice greeted.

“Yes ma’am, May I –”

“You need some help?”

Piper spun around to see Charlie standing behind her with a look of concern on his face. “Oh my tire is..”

“Flat? Yeah, I can help with that.” Charlie replied walking up to examine the tire “ I don’t have my tools with me right now but I can give you a ride to wherever you need to go then I can come back and fix the flat and have the car towed to your Mama’s house.”

“Oh no I don’t want to impose. I’m sure you got things to do Mr. Charlie.” Piper shook her head.

“No imposition at all.” Charlie chortled. “My buddy Earl owns a tow truck and it doesn't take me but five minutes to change a tire. I can have this car back to you in an hour.”

“Ma’am? Hello ma’am are you still in need of assistance?” The operator asked.

“I uh… No, I guess not.” Piper said reluctantly. She thanked the woman then hung up her cell phone then looked up at Charlie.

“Thank you,” she said sincerely.

“No problem.” Charlie opened his truck doors and rushed to get the junk off the bench seat. The kids climbed into the passenger side and Piper climbed in behind them.

“I can’t thank you enough Mr Charlie.”

“Ain’t no problem.”

“Oh cool!” LJ shrieked clasping his cookie stained hand around Charlie’s dog tags hanging from the rearview mirror. Charlie had to resist the urge to smack him silly. Little dummy didn’t even know it was disrespectful to touch a soldier’s dog tags. Those things were an honor.

“Oh Mr. Charlie I didn’t know you served in the military.” Piper acknowledge forming even more respect for him.

“Served 32 years in the army.” Charlie spoke proudly “Retired Sergeant Major. Got these babies and my Purple Heart when we stormed Grenada back in ‘83”

“Wow that sounds exciting!” Piper said casting her eyes out the window

Charlie glanced over at her head full of curls. She was such a natural beauty.
"So how are you settling here in Conners?" He asked barely able to keep his eyes on the road.

"Oh good." Piper replied. "Mama says Dr. Bullock may have a job for me down at the walk-in clinic. She told me to stop by on Monday."

"Oh that sounds like a good start." Charlie nodded. "Dr. Bullock is a good woman to work for. I've known her and her husband for years. She's the breadwinner while he stays at home to watch the kids like he's the wife. They're a bit strange but still good people."

Piper smiled "I hope I get the job. I'm so nervous. I haven't worked a job since high school, aside from being a full-time mom. I hope I don't mess everything up."

"Oh I'm sure you'll do just fine, don't worry about a thing. It'll all work itself out."

"I sure hope so. It's so hard starting over you know." Piper sighed feeling as if the world were on her shoulders.

"I understand."

"Plus I'm just dying to get in my own place.

Don't get me wrong... I love my mother, but now I'm reminded why we can't live together."

The wheels in Charlie's head started to turn.

"Say uh…I got a place if you're interested."

"You do?" Piper's eyes widened.

"It ain't much. A three- bedroom; two bath mobile home not too far from here. It's clean and the rents cheap. I usually ask $450 but I'll let you move in and you can pay me whenever you get on your feet."

"Are you serious?"

"Is that okay?"

"Are you kidding that is amazing! I swear I could just kiss you!"

Charlie smiled to himself. *You don't know how bad I wish I could taste those thick lips of yours, Darling,* he thought. Charlie was in heaven just by being around sweet Piper.

Seven

"You're hired!" Dr. Jamie Lynn Bullock said flatly in a southern drawl.
Piper clutched her resume in her arms and stared awkwardly at the unkempt brunette sitting behind the desk wearing a ketchup stained lab coat. The toys and baby clothes thrown all over made her office resemble more of a nursery than a doctor's office.

"I-I am?" Piper stumbled.

"Sure why not?" Dr. Bullock emphasized with a shrug "You're Pearl's daughter. Charles Brewer put in a good word for you. When can you start Sugar?"

"Well I uh-"

"Hold on a minute!" Dr. Bullock interrupted rushing to soothe the whining infant in the bassinet behind her. Piper watched in bewilderment as Dr. Bullock nonchalantly took out one of her breasts and popped it into the baby's mouth.
"I swear this youngin wants the tit every five minutes!" Dr. Bullock chortled. "He is nothing like my other seven." Dr. Bullock sat back down in her

chair and blew the bangs out of her face. "Ok where were we?"

"You were just asking me when I could start, and I was about to say... I'm sorry did you say you have seven children?"

"Eight!" Dr. Bullock quickly corrected. "Well maybe nine. I'm kinda scared to take the test ya' know. I swear every time Josh looks at me, I get knocked up. I keep telling him we should be on the pill but of course Josh comes from a family of Bible thumpers who believe that birthing babies is all part of God's divine plan. Don't get me wrong Josh does a great job with these youngins but as mother I figure I ought to be more hands on at home which is why I'm needing more help at the office ya' know."

"I see." Piper managed to utter.

"So, when can you start?" Dr Bullock eagerly circled back with her original question.

"I guess I can start tomorrow?"

"Oh thank gawd!" Dr Bullock exclaimed.

The corners of Piper's lips tugged into a smile "Thank you so much for the opportunity Dr. Bullock. I promise to give my new job one hundred and ten percent of my effort."

“Great!” Dr. Bullock raised her brows in fake excitement “Be here at eight o’clock sharp. Kayla, the other medical assistant will show you the ropes. But she leaves for college in a couple of weeks, so I hope you’re a quick learner.”

“Oh, I am Dr. Bullock”

“I prefer to be called Jamie Lynn, Sugar” she cut in. “Dr. Bullock” makes me feel like I’m obligated to be smart and well you know how that goes... I'm sorry do you mind holding him for a sec? I gotta go pee.”

“Um... sure.” Piper replied reluctantly as the bald-headed butter ball of a baby was shoved into her arms.

After the bizarre job interview Piper thanked the Doctor for hiring her and left before she could be asked to change a diaper. The Georgia heat was blazing yet it was a beautiful day outside. Piper was allowing her eyes to adjust to the sun when something caught her eye; The red station wagon parked across the street. This made three times this week she had seen the vehicle. The first time was at her house when she was playing outside with the children. The other time was when she was coming out of the post office. Maybe Piper was going crazy, but she was sure that this car was following her. She squinted to try and make out the shadowy figure behind the windshield. She kept an eye on the station wagon as she popped the lock on her car.

"Hey there good looking!"

Piper spun around to see Deputy Williams standing behind her in his full uniform. "My gawd Yance you scared me!" Piper clutched her chest.

"Oh, my bad." Deputy Williams apologized. "What are you doing up here anyway?"

"I believe I just got myself a job." Piper said unsure of her new position.

"What are you doing here?"

"Weekly cortisone shot in this bum knee." Deputy Williams replied slapping at his right thigh. "Can't be out here running the town crippled."

Piper chuckled. "I heard that old man!"

"Old?" Deputy Williams shrieked. "WOW! Ok since you got jokes how about you let me take you out to lunch so we can celebrate you getting hired."

"I don't know-"

“Listen woman I’m tryna feed you and I’m not taking no for an answer.”

Piper thought about it for a second. “Okay, I guess lunch is fine.”

Eight

Late June bloomed into July. July turned into early August in a blink of an eye for Piper. The sweltering Georgia heat had climbed to the mid 90's and humid as ever. Piper and her kids were finally settling into their new life. It had been a great summer and the kids were excited about starting their first year at a new school. The double wide mobile home that Piper was renting from Mr. Charlie was just perfect for her and the kids. Each one had their own room and the master suite was huge. Mr. Charlie had really played down the property. It was gorgeous and had been upgraded.

"This is really nice Piper." Pearl said looking around Piper's new abode. "I bet you pay big money to live here."

"No, actually the rent is pretty cheap." Piper replied handing her mother a glass of wine. "Plus Mr. Charlie says he will give me a minute to get on my feet and then I can start paying him whatever I can."

"Charlie?" Pearl eyed her daughter with grave concern "You're renting this place from Charles Brewer?"

"I am..." Piper replied slowly. "Okay mama what's wrong with Mr. Charlie? This is the second time you've looked at me crazy when I mentioned his name."

Pearl pondered for a moment, unsure if she should share what was on her heart. Finally, she asked "Do you remember when your daddy died and we were struggling to pay for the funeral?"

"Yes." Piper nodded hesitantly. "We were too busy trying to raise money that we barely had time to mourn. Then in the eleventh hour somebody came through and donated the ten thousand we needed to bury Daddy."

"Well that anonymous donor was Charles Brewer." Pearl groaned. "He showed up to my house one night about a week after the funeral… drunker than Cooter Brown. He had this crazy look in his eyes. He had come there to let me know that he was the one that gave the money and that he was there to collect what I owed him."

"What was that?"

"What you think he was talking about?" Pearl harrumphed with bulging eyes. "I threatened to call the police if he didn't leave my property and luckily, he left. But I'm telling you Piper there is something off about Charlie… something evil deep inside of him. You better be careful accepting anything from him. Make sure he doesn't want more than just the rent from you?"

"He probably was just drunk and made a mistake, Mama." Piper said dismissively. "He hasn't tried anything like that again has he?"

"Well no but-"

"Exactly," Piper quipped. "Mr. Charlie isn't like that. He is a married man who loves his wife to death. I mean why would he even risk ruining his reputation like that. Everyone in this town seems to love him. Plus he's been nothing less than a gentleman in my presence. He even helped me move in and didn't ask me for no booty… He's harmless."

"Well you were never too keen on reading between the lines." Pearl spat irritated by her daughter's naiveté. "Look at who you married!"

"Really mama you not gone let me live that one down, are you?"

"I'm just saying," she shrugged her shoulders. "Just be careful."

"Don't worry I will." Piper said as her eyes fell to the kids playing a board game on the floor.

Pearl let out a sigh. "Well it's getting late and I'm sure you're tired. I'll let you get out of those scrubs and get you some rest."

"Yes ma'am" Piper said. "You're right, morning will be here before you know it.

Piper rose up from the couch stretching her tired muscles before she walked her mother to the door.

"I just want you to know I'm proud of you daughter." Pearl said placing a gentle hand on Piper's cheek lovingly. "You have always been such a strong woman."

"That's me! The strong black woman. "Piper joked raising up a-power-to-the-people fist in the air. They both laughed and Piper watched her mother climb into her Buick and pull off.

"Okay kids time for bed."

Nine

Sweat dripped from Charlie's face as he dug the saw into the burly pig. Crimson hued blood and pinkish guts spilled out onto the concrete floor. Another flock of piggies looked on in horror wondering if they were going to be next. Some old school music played from a nearby car radio. Suddenly the radio announcer announced it was a quarter to seven.

Charlies eyes perked up. "Oh shoot," he mumbled under his breath. He was about to be late. He ran out of the pole barn and across the yard into the house. Ruby was passed out in the Lazy Boy snoring up a storm. A mostly eaten box of Popeyes fried chicken was clutched tight in her chunky hands.

Fat funky bitch! he thought to himself as he eyed her with disgust. He quickly washed himself up and headed back out to the pole barn dressed in a suit and tie; his favorite cup of Bird Dog Cognac was sitting in a glass by his side as he stared at a group of black screens. He took in a deep breath and turned on the monitors. On the first monitor was a view of Piper's living room. He was beginning to notice that Piper wasn't much of a housekeeper.

Two empty wine glasses were sitting on the table. Her mother must've stopped by for a glass of wine. But Piper hadn't even bothered to clean up the glasses which had Charlie a tad bit annoyed. Also, the kids left all their toys on the floor. His issues with Piper's lack of tidiness would have to change if and when he made Piper his woman. He would run a tight ship! The house would need to stay immaculate and the kids would either have to get in order or go live someplace else. That's what he would do… Send the kids to a home; maybe even a military school. Lord knows her kids needed the discipline; especially that smart mouthed little girl.

Charlie flipped the monitor to the kitchen, down the hallway and to the bedrooms until he found Piper in the master bathroom. The shower was already steamy, and he felt himself harden when she walked into the bathroom wrapped in a towel. Her dirty scrubs and underwear were bunched in her hand as she made her way to the hamper. After discarding her dirty garments into the hamper Piper stood in front of the bathroom sink eyeing her reflection in the mirror. The anticipation was built up as Charlie took a swig of his drink to calm the fire burning inside of him. She used a Noxzema pad to cleanse the makeup from her face and brushed her teeth. Then after sucking her gut in and turning side to side she dropped the towel.

"Good gawd almighty!" Charlie wiped the drool from the corners of his mouth as Piper climbed into the shower.

"Oh take your time baby. Daddy got all night." Charlie whispered opening his trousers and grabbing a hold of his slight erection. Her perfect skin, wide hips and perky breast with the chocolate Hershey kissed nipples was enough to drive him over the edge in only thirty seconds. He bent over panting and trying to catch his breath.

"Oh my sweet Piper, I just can't wait to make you all mine."

Ten

Make a right onto Peach Grove Drive then your destination is on the left" the robotic voice of the GPS informed

Piper inched her SUV down the dusty road leading up to the Brewer's residence. A white wooden mailbox with burgundy painted letters spelling out "BREWER" stuck out like a hitchhiker's thumb along the road. Piper pulled up to a white house with burgundy trim that sat peacefully behind a split rail fence. The morning sun cast down on the huge white pole barn that was next to the house.

Guess this is it, Piper thought to herself as she got out and looked around. She walked up to the wooden porch. A Tabby cat was curled up napping lazily on a rocking chair. When it heard Piper's heels hit the concrete pavers, the cat woke up, stretched its gangly body, and then scurried away. ***Ding Dong!***

"Charles get the door!" A female's voice roared, slightly startling Piper.

Moments later the front door yawned, and Charlie's friendly eyes gazed at Piper behind the screen door.

"Piper?" Charlie smiled nervously walking out onto the porch. "W-What brings you by?"

"I was just driving by and decided to bring you this instead of mailing it." Piper reached in her purse and produced a money order. "It's the first month's rent! I just wanted to thank you for all that you've done for me and the kids. We really appreciate you."

"Ahh well you didn't have to go out of your way, Darling." Charlie grinned. "I know times have been rough for you and I don't mind helping. Why don't you keep that money and spend it on you and the kids."

"Mr. Charlie, it's fine. I got a good job and thanks to you- I'm comfortable. Now will you please take my money." Piper playfully twisted her lips.

"Well if you insist!" Charlie finally accepted the money order. His kind eyes squinted as they looked across the yard. Guess I can use this money to get me some new wheels on the backhoe.

Piper followed Charlie's eyes to the rusted-out tractor with the dry rotted tires sitting in the middle of the field.

"My gawd Mr. Charlie!" Piper let out a laugh "Those tires are growing flowers out of them there so old."

"I know." Charlie laughed back. The banter on the front porch caused Ruby to take notice. She sat straight up in her chair.

"Charles!" She hollered. "Who that you talking to?"

An uncomfortable frown formed on Charlie's face. "Nobody Ruby, just a lady stopped by to pay the rent." Charlie hollered back.

"Oh, is that Mrs. Ruby? I haven't seen her in years. Mind if I go inside and say hello?" Piper asked. As if on reflex Charlie threw his hand up blocking Piper's entrance as she tried to walk in the house.

"She's... she's tired. Maybe some other time." He said.

"Oh, I promise, I'll be quick I just want to see her and say hello." Piper insisted.

After careful hesitation Charlie finally relented. "Okay."

The Brewer home was clean, but everything was old. Piper nearly got her heel caught in a tattered area rug as she made her way to the living room. A stench like rotten garbage filled the air when she rounded the corner to the living room. Dimly lit the living room décor of ancient floral patterns greeted her. The drapes had been drawn together only allowing a sliver of light to shine through.

Ruby Brewer sat perched in a lazy boy. The light from the television illuminated the sour puss look on her face. Piper was shocked at the sight of Ruby Brewer. Mrs. Ruby was always a bit of a thick woman, but Piper could barely recognize her now.

"Mrs. Ruby?"

"Who the hell are you?" Ruby grimaced.

"Mrs. Ruby, it's me… Piper. You used to teach my Sunday school class when I was a little girl. I'm Pearl Crosby's daughter."

Ruby squinted her eyes into narrow slits and kissed her teeth. "Pearl Crosby! Humph, figures Pearl's daughter would be the one skinning and grinning all up in my husband's face. Like mother, like daughter. What are you doing here anyway?" Ruby's rude reaction surprised Piper.

She slid her eyes to Charlie who seemed to be dying of embarrassment then turned back to Ruby. "I came to bring my rent payment."

“Dressed like that?” Ruby spat looking her up and down in disgust.

“Umm…” Feeling naked suddenly Piper subconsciously tugged at the hem of her skirt wishing it was a bit longer.

“Well did you give my husband your rent payment?”

“Yes ma’am.”

“Well then, I guess you should be on your way, huh?”

“Yes ma’am.”

“Charlie show her the door. And sweetheart you can mail the rent payments from now on. Charlie tries to be spirit filled but he has a weak mind. He doesn’t need any half naked women around him blocking his blessings... You be blessed now.”

“Yes, ma’am you too.” Piper was at a loss for words as she headed for the door.

“I’m sorry about that.” Charlie murmured his apologies as he escorted Piper outside. “I tried to tell you she was tired.”

“It’s okay really.” Piper quickly said now wishing she had taken heed. “Thanks so much Mr. Charlie I’ll see you around. And please let your wife know that I never meant any disrespect.”

Ruby snatched opened the drapes and watched the beautiful young woman climb into her SUV and pull out of the yard. As soon as Piper’s SUV disappeared from sight Ruby frowned up her face. “Jezebel!” She hissed.

Eleven

*L*ife for Piper was slowly coming together for the good. The new job was better than she imagined at the clinic. Her kids were adjusting quite well, and she even was starting to become independent. As the kids sat at the dining room table giggling and eating grilled cheese sandwiches Piper put away the laundry. Her week had been exhaustingly busy at the clinic and she barely had any time to herself, let alone get any housework done. Her first Saturday off she took the opportunity to wash the mounds of clothes accumulating in the hampers and clean up thoroughly.

Making her way from room to room Piper paused when she noticed something strange about her laundry. Despite washing every stitch of clothing she owned, she still seemed to be missing several pairs of underwear from her panty drawer.

"What in the world?" She mumbled sifting through the half empty drawer. Even the new bra sets she had just purchased were gone.

Other strange happenings had been occurring in her new home as well. Sometimes she would arrive home to find that her dishes had been washed or the kids' toys had been put away. One time she came home, all the beds were made, and the home was completely spotless. She immediately called her mother.

"No, I haven't been there." Pearl had insisted. The revelation caused the hairs on the back of Piper's neck to stand at attention. Someone had been inside her house. Someone had access to her and her babies. But who?

Piper had quickly phoned the police and made a report. Deputy Williams assured her he would investigate the matter and even volunteered to spend a couple of nights on her couch so that she and the kids would feel safe.

Strangely enough after Piper filed the police report the break ins seemed to stop. But now her panties were missing. Piper was about to investigate further when she heard a loud CRASH coming from the kitchen. She dashed down the hallway to find LJ standing on the kitchen counter and one of her good glasses shattered on the floor along with a pitcher of red juice spilled out on the kitchen floor.

"What the hell are you doing?" Piper shrieked.

"Trying to get us some juice." LJ mumbled. His wide eyes displayed his befuddlement.

"I told him to ask you, Mama." Phoebe tattled with her hands on her hips. "But that boy doesn't ever listen."

After cleaning up the mess and sending the kids both to their rooms thirsty, Piper carried a hefty trash bag out to the garbage. The sun was out but it wasn't as hot given that the weather had headed into September.

Piper dragged the heavy bag out to her fence line where the small dumpster she shared with the family across the street was. Conners didn't have city trash pick-up like when Piper was living in Atlanta. Most people in the tiny rural town usually hauled their own trash to the city dump or paired up with the neighbors to share the cost of having the city dump provide a dumpster.

Out of the corner of her eyes Piper saw the red station wagon sitting at the edge of her driveway. Her heart began to pound in her chest. Why was this car following her? She decided to find out.

"Hey!" Piper waved as she rushed up to the station wagon.

The station wagon immediately started the engine and drove away… but not before Piper could grab the license plate number.

Twelve

*T*he Conners Day picnic was always the rave around Conners. Patrons from Podunk towns far and wide showed up to celebrate the history of the Conners Plantation. Many families, tourist, and elected officials were all in attendance. This was a day for celebration for colored folk.

Conners was once owned by George Conners who started the small plantation in 1798. When he died he left all the land he owned and his money to his best slave; also named George. George was described as being Mulatto; both black and white. There was once speculation on who George's daddy was but after the will stated Mulatto George as the sole heir in ol' man Conners' will the rumors were quickly laid to rest along with old man Conners.

Mulatto George then went on to establish a town out of the land. Every year downtown main street was transformed into a festival for the whole town to enjoy.

"No! No! Josh Jr. don't hit your brother with that! Emma Belle you're supposed to eat the ice cream cone, not wear it! Where is yawls Daddy?" Jamie Lynn fussed; wrangling her kids while they ran around like wild animals. She pushed the double stroller up to the booth of homemade jams.

Piper was working with her mother Pearl packaging jams for display. Jamie Lynn collapsed on the table almost tipping the jars over.

"Ugh… Anybody want some slightly used kids? I'm running a two for one special… No exchanges or returns!"

Piper chuckled at her boss while she breathed a sigh of relief. She and Jamie Lynn had really become close. So close that besides being on a first name basis, they hung out often outside of work. Turns out Piper went to school with Jamie Lynn's husband Josh. Piper had always known Josh as a shy timid little mama's boy. Who knew he would grow up to be the baby making horn-dog that he was?

"Sorry, Jamie Lynn." Piper laid a gentle hand on her friend's shoulder. "I have a two-kid limit in my house."

"Don't even think about looking at me." Pearl quipped scooping the baby from the stroller and kissing his cheek. "Besides you're a doctor? Don't you know how these cute little rug rats are made?"

"Oh, I know how they're made alright." Jamie Lynn giggled slyly as she rubbed on her small baby bump. “Sure is a lot of fun making ‘em. It’s the raising them part that’s fixing on sending me to the crazy house!”

“Mama! Mama! Can Josh Jr and I go dunk Mr. Charlie?” L.J. asked running up to the booth.

“Don’t forget me! I wanna go dunk Mr. Charlie too.” Phoebe whined.

“How about we all go dunk Mr. Charlie!” Jamie Lynn through her arms up. “Let’s tire you young’ins out so maybe y’all will sleep tonight. Daddy and me, can have some alone time.” She aimed a finger at Piper knowing she was about to say something. “Shut up.”

Piper giggled and shook her head; casting her eyes across the courtyard. Charlie was clad in a clown wig and makeup. His sky-blue swimming trunks were pulled high above his large belly; almost touching his breastbone. He looked a bit wobbly as he got help from Deputy Williams to climb into the dunk tank. Piper held in her laughter until she and the crew had made their way over to the dunk tank.

“Mr. Charlie what on earth are you doing up there?” Piper laughed. Mr. Charlie laughed too thinking that Piper looked so pretty in her yellow sundress.

"I don't even know myself," he chuckled. "Pastor and First Lady hoodwinked me into doing this."

"I'm gonna dunk you Mr. Charlie!" L.J. shouted excitedly.

"You can try it if you dare!" Charlie laughed heartily.

The dunk booth was becoming a popular site as all the kids gathered around for their chance to dunk Mr. Charlie. The first round of kids failed miserably. And Mr. Charlie bragged proudly still dry.

"Better luck next time!" Charlie taunted them as they walked away with their heads hung low. Josh Jr. gave up and threw a temper tantrum after the first try then it was L.J.'s turn.

"Come on LJ!" Piper and Jamie Lynn cheered him on. LJ threw his first bean bag which fell way short. That was the warm-up.

"Ha!" Mr. Charlie taunted.

LJ took another shot which was closer but not close enough. The last bean bag Piper asked him for. Winding her arm up Piper teased Mr. Charlie.

“All right Mr. Charlie lets see you make fun of this!” Piper shouted. *BING!*

The bean bag hit the bullseye and Charlie went splashing into the pool. Flopping around like a fish out of water, Charlie looked like he was about to drown. Piper sort of felt sorry for him. The crowd erupted into laughter as kids teased Mr. Charlie.

“Are you okay Mr. Charlie?” She helped him out the dunk tank and handed him a towel.

“Oh, ain’t nothing to it. Just a little Charlie horse... Get it? Charlie horse” he said.

Piper shook her head smiling then rushed to hand Charlie his eyeglasses. He touched her hand when he took the glasses and warm electricity shot up his spine. There was a split second when he was staring at her awkwardly.

“Well I sure am hungry” Piper smiled politely while moving a stray hair out of her face.

“The ribs should be just about done.” Charlie informed. “I want you to try this new recipe I’m trying for the BBQ sauce anyway.”

“I’ll be glad to. Cause the way my stomach mumbling your good ol' ribs would satisfy this hunger." Piper smiled.

Under the gazebo in the courtyard the bass reverberated house music from two Alpine speakers. Jamie Lynn, Phoebe, L.J. and Josh Jr. all started dancing. The festival was now in full swing.

"Hey let's dance!" Deputy Williams suddenly appeared, pulling Piper by the hand.

"Oh, I love to dance" Piper snapped her fingers. "Let's go!"

There was a noticeable uncomfortable shift in Charlie when he saw the deputy. "Y'all go head." He said solemnly. "I gotta get to the smoker."

"Awww, Mr. Charlie those ribs will be fine- you wanna dance?" Piper asked looking at him.

"Oh no Darling I can't." Charlie shook his head.

"Come on old man!" Deputy Williams slapped Charlie's shoulder. "Gone sho' that young gal what an old man can do."

Charlie looked around "I dunno."

"Mr. Charlie don't tell me your chicken." Jamie Lynn taunted. "Bock, Bock, Booooock!"

"It's okay if you're too scared to dance with me Mr. Charlie" Piper smiled swaying her hips to the beat. "I'll just have to dance with Yance."

"I ain't scared. I'll dance with you." Charlie quickly said rushing to get in front of Deputy Williams. They all made their way to a crowd of people already dancing.

"Oh man there's Mr. Charlie y'all" the DJ shouted. "Let's play something special just for you."

The beat dropped to Mr. Cheeks' smash hit song "Lights Camera Action."

Uh shorty, turn it around lemme see somethin'

Messing with me for real, it's gone be somethin'

Yea, I'm talking Light Camera Action

Had me singin', I'm sorry Miss Jackson

Charlie danced his heart out twisting his old body and letting loose. Everyone was watching him cut up. Charlie had showed out and taught the youngins a thing or two.

When they were done Charlie was dog tired. He grabbed his hand towel and rested against a tree to catch his breath. “Whew… Not bad for an old man huh?” He spoke between breaths.

“No not at all I bet you were the cat’s meow back in the day.” Piper teased.

Charlie looked around noticing they were alone. This was his moment to tell Piper what he was feeling. “Uh Piper there is something I’ve been meaning to tell you.”

“Yes.” She looked at him with her amazing brown eyes and his words somehow got stuck in his throat.

“Well...”

“What is it Mr. Charlie?” She stroked his hand and looked into his eyes.

“Well what I’ve been meaning to tell you is…"

“You can tell me anything." Piper assured him.

“Well what I’ve been meaning to tell you is... what I’ve been meaning to say is-" Mr. Charlie stammered struggling to find a way to tell her how he felt.

“You motherfucka!”

Both Piper and Charlie whipped their heads around to see an older woman staring at Charlie. Her dark brown skin melted into some baby fine hair she kept neatly pulled back in a ponytail. She had high cheekbones and a surly crazed look in her eyes. She was petite but her presence was humongous.

"Umm, is everything okay?" Piper stood up and darted her eyes between the woman and Charlie.

"I'm afraid I don't know who this woman is." Charlie said nervously.

The woman narrowed her eyes into slits. "You're a got damn lie! You know me and you for sure know my daughter. I wanna know what you did to my baby Charlie! What did you do?"

"I don't know what you are talking about!" Charlie insisted becoming embarrassed.

"Liar!" The lady lunged at Charlie holding a knife.

"Stop it! Stop! Piper screamed. "Yance!" She yelled causing even more folks to stare as the Deputy Williams ran over and wrestled the woman to the ground pulling the knife out of her hand. She screamed obscenities at Charlie even after she was placed in handcuffs and placed in the backseat of a police cruiser.

“Are you okay Mr. Charlie?” Piper asked looking confused.

“Yes, I'm alright.” Charlie replied leveling an evil glare at his attacker as the police took her away to the jail house.

“Want to tell me what that was about?” Piper stared at him inquisitively.

“I think her name is Margaret. Her daughter Teresa used to be one of my tenants. She was out of rehab and trying to get her life together. I tried to help her out with a place to stay and money but she wanted more. I think the drugs might’ve fried her brain because she was always trying to seduce me. I told her I was married and I love my Ruby and that's when she just lost it. Started going crazy. Then finally she swallowed a bunch of pills and fell asleep in the bathtub. Her parents blame me. I just never could forgive myself.” Mr. Charlie began to wail like a newborn baby needing its mother.

Piper took him in and embraced him. “It’s okay Mr. Charlie I’m here for you.”

Thirteen

*T*he Conner's clinic was always packed to capacity given that it was the only walk in clinic in a forty-mile radius. Piper had gotten herself into a routine. Working for Dr. Jamie Lynn Bullock was challenging but there was never a dull moment.

"Piper we got ourselves a gusher in room three! Get me the four by four gauze, the stitch kit, and a shit ton of saline stat!" Jamie Lynn came barreling through the clinic like a bull in a China shop.

"Right away" Piper nodded, scrambling to her feet.

The morning went by at the speed of lightning and Piper could finally take a little break before the afternoon rush. She let out a deep sigh as she melted into her chair, closing her eyes to relieve the migraine that was threatening to come. The phone rang.

"Good afternoon, Dr. Bullock's office. How may I help you?" Piper greeted the caller.

"Roses are red, they stank a whole bunch, I'm broke and hungry... can you take me to lunch?"

Piper rolled her eyes heavenward and chuckled. “That was super corny, Yance.”

“But did it work? Can you treat a brother to some food?”

“All you think about is eating!”

“Not true. I also think about you... Well I think about eating you... so I guess you’re right.”

“Yance!”

“Sorry... My bad just telling the truth.”

Piper sucked in a small breath blushing. “I’ll meet you at Burger Barn in ten minutes.”

“Bet! See you there!”

Piper hung up the phone smiling to herself as she grabbed her purse and keys. She poked her head in Dr. Bullock's office.

“I’m headed to Burger Barn, you want anything."

“Ooh can you get me a number two extra sauce.” Jamie Lynn replied stuffing a crumpled up twenty in Pipers hand. “Tons of extra sauce! I want my burger to be drowning in sauce!”

“Got it!” Piper made her way out the front door but was surprised to see Charlie on the other side.

“Hey Mr. Charlie.” Piper’s brows knitted together. “We just closed the clinic down for lunch. We open back up at 1 o’clock.”

“I know” Charlie said with a wide toothed smile. He lifted up a plastic bag with a Styrofoam container seated inside. In his opposite hand he carried a Styrofoam cup full of sweet iced tea “I brought you lunch.”

“Well that was nice of you, but I’m already headed out to go meet Yance for lunch. Why didn’t you call first?”

The friendly smile Charlie wore quickly disappeared. “I wanted to surprise you, Darling.” He replied sweetly. “I wanted to apologize for that mishap at the festival. I wanted to thank you for being there for me. Where y’all going to eat?”

“Nothing fancy just the Burger Barn.” Piper answered. “And there is no need for you to apologize. We can just-”

“I went through all this trouble to bring you a hot lunch and you’d rather have some funky ass

Burger Barn!" His venomous words stunned Piper. The look on his face frightened her even more.

"First of all, don't you ever speak to me like that." Piper stood her ground. "Secondly, I never asked you to bring me anything. And thirdly you have a nice damn day, Charlie!" Piper attempted to storm off, but Charlie grabbed her by the arm.

"Don't you walk away from me." He gritted.

"What is wrong with you? Get your goddamn hands off of me! Let me go! Mr. Charlie let me go! I said let me-"

"What in the hell is going on out here? "Jamie Lynn boomed after she snatched open the front door to the office. Charlie quickly released his grip on Piper's arm and tried to explain.

"Nothing." He stumbled. "I just uh-"

"I think you'd better leave Charlie." Jamie Lynn said firmly, her arms folded across her chest. They both glared at Charlie until he had climbed back into his truck and sped off.

"Dammit Charlie you done gone and did it now!" The voice inside Charlie's head chastised him. "Keep it up and she will end up just like the last one."

“No, she won’t!” Charlie slammed his hand hard against the steering wheel. “I’m going to fix this somehow... I promise.”

Fourteen

*I*t was a beautiful Sunday morning and Mr. Charlie was eager to get to church early. Piper would be there. He put his finest suit on and was sure to wear his best cologne. He couldn't wait to get Piper alone so that he could apologize to her. She had to understand that he didn't mean what he said. Yes, it was all just a big misunderstanding.

"Ya' dressing mighty snazzy for church don't ya' think!" Ruby spat bitterly from her lazy boy. She eyed him suspiciously and scratched her scalp through her bonnet.

"No." Charlie defended. "I always get dressed up to go to the house of the Lord."

Ruby harrumphed. She twisted her soup cooler lips and landed her hazel eyes back to the Joel Osteen program that was playing on the television. Then she had an idea. "Charlie!"

"Yes Ruby?" Charlie groaned.

"Get my good chair out the cellar."

"For what My Love?"

"Because I'm going to church with you."

Charlie paused in the middle of the hallway, back peddled and poked his head into the living room. "Come again?"

"You heard me" Ruby snapped. "Go get my good chair out the cellar, and make sure you put a little baby oil in the water when you bring my wash bucket."

"But Ruby, morning service starts in an hour. You know I gots to get there early. It's going to take an hour and a half just to get you ready."

"Well instead of running your trap I suggest you get on it."

"But Ruby-"

"Charlie what kinda fool do you take me for? I know that ol' Jezebel with her two kids will be there at the church. I know she got you hypnotized and under her spell. Now my momma once told me that a man is like a tiger. Woman dangle her meat in front of him long enough, sooner or later he gone take a bite. I have to be there sometimes to remind you that I am a steak and two-bit hussies like Piper Jackson are rotten fish."

"Yes, My Love" Charlie grumbled and headed towards the cellar. *Fat Funky Bitch!*

Two hours later they arrived church was rocking. Tambourines slammed against calloused hands as everyone rejoiced in the glory of the Lord. Charlie was miserable. Plus, there was no sign of his beloved Piper.

It had been awhile since the church had seen Ruby. A lot of churchgoers offered fake smiles and pretended not to notice her struggle for air. Others whispered about how big she had gotten as they tried their best not to stare at her. Ruby didn't seem to notice all the gawking as she sat in her wheelchair parked at the outside aisle of the first row. A giant pink hat with a thin veal covered her round face. Her arms looked like ham shanks as she clapped her hands together and sang along with the choir.

Suddenly the doors to the sanctuary opened. Charlie sat up on the edge of his seat. *Is it her? Please let it be her*. The wind was let out of Charlie's sails as he watched Pearl Crosby walk in with Piper's two kids but no Piper.

Where was she? He looked around the sanctuary and noticed that Deputy Williams was also absent from this morning's service. His chest began to tighten. He had taken two of his blood pressure medications, but it didn't seem to be enough.

She's avoiding you. Probably out somewhere having a good time with that young Deputy... Told you done messed up... you big dummy" the voice inside his head was starting to sound a lot like Ruby.

"Shut up" he hissed.

"Whatcha say brother?"

Charlie looked up to see Deacon Sims eyeing him with a level of concern etched across his tan freckled face. "You Okay Deacon Brewer?"

"Yes." Charlie squeaked out; large beads of sweat now pouring down his face. His suit was starting to feel too tight. "I think my pressure up again. Need to go get my pills out of the car."

Charlie felt extremely lightheaded and dizzy on his way to the car. Once he got outside the world around him started spinning. The last thing he remembered was clutching his chest before falling out on the church lawn.

###

Piper sat on the edge of the lake watching the water. It was a peaceful place that she could go and clear her mind. Charlie had been trying desperately to apologize to her but she ignored his calls and avoided him at all cost.

“Oh, I think I got one!” Deputy Williams broke Piper’s train of thought as he yanked on his fishing pole; reeling in a nice sized brim fish.

“Looka there! Ya' boy got him a big ol' fish.” Deputy Williams celebrated. When he noticed Piper wasn’t celebrating with him, he let out a sigh and set his fishing pole down.

“Okay, it's not that big of a fish” he took Pipers small hands into his and looked her deeply in the eyes. “What’s wrong with you?”

“Nothing” Piper looked away. Deputy Williams cupped her chin in his hands and offered her a knowing look.

“You’re lying.” He said flatly. “There has to be an explanation for you wanting us to skip church and driveway out here in the middle of nowhere on this good Sunday morning.”

“Okay, okay!” Piper finally relented. “Do you remember the other day when we were supposed to meet up for lunch at the Burger Barn and I canceled on you at the last minute?”

“Yeah” Deputy Williams nodded. “You told me you felt sick.”

"Yes, well I wasn't sick." Piper shook her head and sighed hard. "Mr. Charlie showed up to my job as I was leaving. We had a brief conversation and when things didn't go Mr. Charlie's way… he umm… he sort of… attacked me."

"He what?" Deputy Williams glared with his brows knitted together; a noticeable rise in his chest as his pace quickened. "He attacked you?"

"Don't worry Jamie Lynn and I handled the situation and he left but it was something about him that disturbed me. It's like he just snapped and turned into a whole other person."

Deputy Williams searched Piper's eyes for a while then looked out onto the water.

"Well you know… Mr. Charlie was in the military for most of his life. Even when he and Ruby first came to Conners he was off on deployment all the time; fighting in wars and stuff. The man has been through a lot. Probably seen a lot too. Mrs. Ruby had told the ladies at the church that Mr. Charlie suffers from PTSD."

"Well that explains a lot" Piper harrumphed.

"Now I feel bad for avoiding him."

"Something else you've been avoiding too." Deputy Williams slipped a strong arm around Piper's waist and drew her close.

"What's that?" Piper smirked.

"Isn't it obvious?" Deputy Williams raised his brow. "I'm tryna make you mine and you keep playing me to the left."

"No, I'm not!"

"Well what's the holdup then? When we gonna make this thing between us official?"

Piper rolled her eyes and sighed. "I don't know… I just been through a lot and I'm not trying to rush into anything else right now."

"Well we ain't gotta rush. We can take our time. As long as you promise not to hold what your ex husband did to you against me and give me a chance."

"I promise." Piper agreed smiling as she admired his smooth silky skin.

"Seal it with a kiss?"

“Boy you think you slick.” Piper giggled but still allowed his soft brown lips to caress hers in a warm passionate kiss.

Suddenly Deputy Williams’ walkie talkie started to squawk with a female’s voice.

“Deputy Williams do you copy?” The female dispatcher asked.

Deputy Williams unclipped his walkie talkie and spoke into it “Deputy Williams here. What’s up?”

“Requesting a police escort for the ambulance into Albany.”

“Escort for what? What happened?”

There was a long pause before the dispatcher finally said, “Charles Brewer had a heart attack this morning.”

"Oh my God!" Piper shouted.

Fifteen

Piper rode shotgun alongside Deputy Williams as an ambulance followed them into Albany. Piper's mind raced a mile a minute. After Yance told her about Charlie's PTSD she couldn't help but feel sorry for him. She hated for anything serious to happen to him knowing that he was the sole caretaker of his wife Ruby.

The hospital in Albany was bustling with activity when Piper and Deputy Williams arrived. Deputy Williams parked his police cruiser at the entrance of the Emergency room, he and Piper got out.

"May I help you officer?" a nurse with a friendly face asked Deputy Williams when he walked in.

"Yes, I just escorted Charles Brewer from Conners" Deputy Williams replied. "Do you know which way they took him?"

The nurse looked Charlie up in the computer. "They just took him to the second floor operating room" she replied. "I'll get one of the transporters to show you where the waiting room is for open heart recovery."

After a couple of hours, Piper and Yance were allowed inside to see Charlie. He was hooked up to all kinds of I.V.'s and monitors. His skin was an ashy grey. The doctor said that he underwent a triple heart bypass and the road to recovery would be long.

"Look at ya' old man trying to tap out on me." Deputy Williams walked up to Charlie's bedside with a smile on his face.

Charlie opened his eyes; smiled and whispered weakly. "I ain't old."

"You tell 'em Mr. Charlie." Piper quipped

Charlie looked over to see Piper standing over him and his heart swelled with excitement.

"No Mr. Charlie don't try to get up." Piper said noticing he was struggling to sit up. "Just rest." She put her hand on his warm forehead and caressed it.

Charlie motioned at his neck. The breathing tube that the surgeons had inserted during the open-heart surgery left his throat raw.

"You want some water?" Deputy Williams asked.

Mr. Charlie nodded. The pitcher next to Charlie's bed was empty. "I'ma go find him some water." Deputy Williams said disappearing into the hallway leaving Piper alone with Charlie.

Charlie making sure the coast was clear gazed into her eyes.

"How are you feeling Mr. Charlie?" Piper asked.

His lips started moving frantically, but nothing was coming out.

"What was that?" Piper leaned in closer to hear him.

"What the hell are you doing to my husband Jezebel!"

Piper spun around to see Ruby Brewer in the doorway glaring at her while sitting in the wheelchair. A couple of the female church members also gave Piper the stank eyes as they followed Ruby into the room.

"Umm I was just-"

"I know what you were doing heffa!" Ruby snarled. "I've been knowing what you been doing. You're trying to steal my man."

“What?” Piper shrieked. “It's nothing like that Mrs. Ruby.”

“I want you to know I serve a might-ty gawd who sits high and looks low. He sees the evildoers of this world and he will shut you down homewrecker! Now I’m gonna give you one and only one warning to stay away from my husband or else!” Ruby’s double chin jiggled as she screamed at the top of her lungs.

“What’s going on in here?” Deputy Williams asked as he walked in carrying a full container of water.

“Nothing” Piper shook her head. “Can we just go please.”

Charlie’s eyes were dancing wildly as he watched the confrontation between his wife and Piper. Thank heavens for Deputy Williams returning when he did.

"Why? We just got here." Deputy Williams said glancing between Piper and Mrs. Ruby.

"Well this homewrecker isn't welcomed here. You can stay as long as you like Deputy." Mrs. Ruby spat.

"Now wait a minute sister Ruby, why the disrespect for Piper. Her and I came together to see about Mr. Charlie. No need to act that way." Deputy Williams fussed at Mrs. Ruby.

"Trust me, that Jezebel been after my Charlie! I'm watching her." Ruby hissed rolling her eyes at Piper.

"I don't have to stay. I'll be down stairs waiting." Piper said leaving out brushing past the sisters from the church.

Sixteen

Several weeks later Charlie had made a full recovery with a new lease on life. Suffering a major heart attack really put things in perspective for him. The hand of God had come down hard on him. Making him realize he needed to get his house in order, stop wasting time.

Piper was his number one priority from now on. No sense in keeping his true feelings hidden any longer it was time Piper knew.

Charlie had lied to Ruby telling her he was headed into town to the general store to pick up his medications. Instead he made a b-line for the mobile home. He pulled his truck into the driveway behind Piper's SUV truck and parked. The pressure building in Charlie nerves threatened to get the best of him.

Checking his surroundings, he surveyed the house. It appeared that Piper and the kids were at home alone. Gathering his nerves Charlie removed the small jar of Vaseline and lubed up his dry cracked lips. *Go get her, and don't screw up!* It was now or never.

The fall air had sent a gust of wind into Piper's cracked window. She moved her face finding a cool spot on her pillow and nestled back into a deep slumber. Then the sudden sound of her kid's laughter caused her to reopen her eyes. She looked over at the night stand. The clock read 8:36 in the morning. She let out a hard sigh yawning before stretching her limbs.

It was a crisp chilly Saturday. She was hoping the kids would let her sleep in until at least 10:00am. Frustrated Piper climbed out of bed and tossed on a robe. She could smell bacon frying and hear the kids squealing all the way down the hallway. Assuming her mother had come over to cook breakfast she smiled.

The hairs on the back of her neck prickled instantly. What she saw once she rounded the corner caused her to stop dead in her tracks. The house was immaculate; not a thing out of place. Every dish was washed, dried, and put up. All the kid's toys were put away. Each surface had been dusted and wiped down. Besides the aroma of food, the smell of pine, and bleach tickled her nose.

How long had he been in her house? "Mr. Charlie?" Piper asked confused.

Clad in an apron that read “South In Ya' Mouth” Charles Brewer stood comfortably at the stove scrambling eggs humming a tune.

“Oh, hey there, Darling.” He smiled; his gold tooth blinging as he turned his attention back to the stove. “You’re just in time for breakfast.”

“What are you doing here?” Piper asked firmly with her hand on her hip.

“I was just passing through and thought maybe you and the kids might want a nice breakfast to get your day started.”

“You can’t just show up to my home like this Mr. Charlie!”

“Your home?” Charlie chuckled. “With all due respect Darling the last time I checked it was my name on the deed to this here property.”

Piper’s eyes nearly popped outside her head. She could feel herself about to go off but then she remembered that there were two little people in the room watching them both.

“Can we talk outside” she said through gritted teeth.

Piper was livid when she stomped out to the porch. Charlie right behind.

“Okay” Piper let out a sigh. “First of all, let me just say that I’m happy you made a full recovery.”

“Well thank you Darling” Charlie smiled.

“But Mr. Charlie there has to be some boundaries here.”

“Boundaries?” Charlie’s brows knotted together.

“First of all, don’t ever pop up on me and my family unannounced. My own mama doesn’t even do that. You need to call first. Regardless if it is your house, I pay my rent on-time and in full, respect my privacy."

Charlie’s jaw clenched. “I understand.”

“Secondly, I’m not sure what the hell you and your wife got going on but for some reason she is under the impression that I’m after you and I’m not! You need to fix that immediately. I’ve been through a lot these last few months and the last thing I need is-”

“I know that Darling. And that’s why I’m here.”

Piper looked at Charlie puzzled. Stepping back some to put good enough distance between them she allowed him to speak.

"When I was laying up in that hospital, I realized how close I came to dyin'. I could hear the voice of God telling me it's time. It's time for me to finally be happy... and I want to do that with the woman that makes me happy."

"Mr. Charlie what are you talking about?"

"I'm talking about us" he said in a matter-of-fact manner.

"Me and you together. I'm trying to make you my wife. I want to take care of you and love you forever... I suppose I can take care of the kids too."

"Wait! What?" Piper threw her hands in the air to silence him as she tried to choke down the vomit bubbling at the back of her throat. "Whoa! Just wait a damn minute. Now Mr. Charlie if I gave you the wrong impression then I'm sorry but there is absolutely no way in hell that I could ever... that *we* could ever. First of all I'm not looking to be in a relationship but even if I was... You are like a father figure to me, Mr. Charlie. I don't see you as anything else. I really hope you can understand that."

Charlie's eyes glossed over behind his eyeglasses. Piper wasn't sure if he was angry or sad. The sudden silence was deafening.

"I understand" he finally said with emptiness in his eyes. He reached into his front pocket, retrieved a toothpick, stuck it in his mouth and walked away.

Piper watched Charlie climb in his truck and drive off before she finally let out a sigh. She stormed inside the house and yelled for the kids to come here.

"Yes mama?" LJ rounded the corner with Phoebe on his heels.

"Listen to me." Piper addressed the both of them with sternness. "If anyone comes to this house you better come get me. Don't you open that door for anyone except your grandmother do you two understand me?"

"Yes ma'am" they both nodded.

"But mama" Phoebe said "We didn't open the door for Mr. Charlie. He let himself in... He had a key!"

Seventeen

"Ha-ha! You thought she would fall in love with you. Boy don't you look stupid. I bet she's going to tell everybody what you just did. You just look like a big ass fool!"

"Shut up! Shut up!" Charlie screamed at the voice inside his head. Tears flowed down his cheeks mixed with the snot that ran from his nose as he sped down the street. "She does love me she just needs to be reminded of what I can do for her! And she's not gone tell nobody what I said. She's not like that."

"She's a whore! You heard her. She gave you boundaries. And now she gone tell everybody you came on to her. Ha-ha!"

"I know, I know. I just got to get to her some other kind of way."

"How?" Charlie drove his truck in his yard and killed the engine. He rested his aching head on the steering wheel and felt his chest tighten.

What could he do? What could he do to make her understand that he loved her? How can he make her pay attention? He was sure she was somewhere running her mouth about their encounter. He needed to flip the script on her but how? The drapes shifted in the window. *Ruby*, he thought to himself. *That's how I'll do it.*

Ruby was in the middle of watching her pre recorded soap operas. She had just double dipped a Ruffles plain potato chip into a jar of French onion dip when she heard the front door flung open.

"Ruby!" Charlie screamed repeatedly. "Ruby!"

"What you want negro?" Ruby snapped. "What's your problem calling my name like this here? What happened to you?"

"Oh Ruby" Charlie collapsed on Ruby's lap and withstood the foul odor seeping in between her legs.

"What you want Charles? Nigga get off me!"

"Ruby you were right!" Charlie wept. "That Piper Jackson ain't nothing but an ol' Jezebel like you said."

"What? What happened?"

"Well I went to her house to collect my rent money."

“You told me you were going to get your medication.” Ruby looked at him skeptical.

“I know but since she hadn’t paid the whole time I was in the hospital, I figured I would go by and collect the rent ya' know. When I get over there those poor children said they were hungry. Oh Ruby, they hadn’t eaten in days and the house was filthy. So I find whatever I could and make them breakfast. Piper finally wakes up and come out the bedroom in nothing but her nightclothes. She got this look in her eyes like she wanted me. I tell her I’m uncomfortable and she can go fetch the rent while I wait outside. She follows me and says she ain’t got no rent money. She says she want to pay another way.”

“What?” Ruby shrieked; her eyes peeled back with shock.

“I told her I’m not that kind of man and that’s when she told me I was going to be with her or else.... Oh Ruby what am I gonna do? She threatened to tell people I came onto her.”

The wheels inside of Ruby Brewers head began to turn. “We’ll just see about that.” She spat. “Charlie hand me that phone.”

As Charlie watched Ruby dial up the numbers, the corners of his mouth twisted up in a sinister smile. Piper was going to learn her place and learn it quick.

"Hello Johnnie Mae." Ruby snarled into the phone. "Let me tell you what that Jezebel has done to my Charlie."

###

"*I* think you might be overreacting a little bit. "Deputy Williams said looking at all the dead bolt lock kits in Piper's basket.

"No, I'm not" Piper shook her head. "I'm telling you that man has been in my house when I'm not there I just know it."

"Are you sure?"

"Yes!" Piper hissed; her eyes gazing around the hardware store. "I'm sure of it. I gotta change the locks as soon as possible. You should've seen the look in his eyes."

They made their way to the front checkout counter. "Will this be all?" the clerk asked smiling at Deputy Williams.

"Yes" Piper answered for him. The Clerk glared at Piper.

"I was talking to Deputy Williams." She spat rudely.

"Well excuse the hell out of me" Piper drew her face up in a frown.

They completed their transaction and the clerk continued to glare at Piper. "Is there something you need to say to me?" Piper asked

"No" the clerk scoffed. "Just wanted to see what a home wrecking heffa looked like close up."

"Excuse me!"

"It's a shame what you doing to Mr. Charlie. He and his wife are good people."

"What?" Piper furrowed her brows. "What have I done to Charlie?"

The woman just stood there glaring at Piper, not saying anything at all. Piper tried not to let the woman's words affect her but she would soon notice that the store clerk wasn't the only one who had a problem with her.

Some of the patients at the clinic refused to allow Piper to triage them. The ladies at the church offered her the stank-eye whenever she walked into the sanctuary.

The bad vibes were proving to be too much. Piper decided to ask Jamie Lynn about it while taking their kids out to the Conners Corn Maze and Pumpkin Patch one evening in mid-October.

"Can I ask you a question?" Piper said to Jamie after noticing the man at the concession stand had failed to smile when he handed her back her change.

"Yeah what is it?" Jamie Lynn blew on her funnel cake before taking a huge bite out of it. Piper casted her eyes out to Deputy Williams and Jamie Lynn's husband Josh helping the kids pick out pumpkins for jack o lanterns as she and Jamie Lynn scrolled up to the corn maze.

"Are people talking about me?" Piper asked flatly.

"What do you mean people? What people?"

"People!" Piper's eyes bulged. "Are they talking about me."

Jamie Lynn hesitated for a moment. "Well there are some rumors going around that you tried to sleep with Charles Brewer."

"What?!"

“But those are just rumors started by Ruby. Don’t worry about her lard ass. She’s just old and miserable.”

Piper’s mouth flung open “Did you just call Mrs. Ruby a lard ass?”

“I sure as hell did.” Jamie Lynn quipped. “You know it’s the truth!”

“I can’t with you!” Piper laughed.

“She’s probably sitting on her couch right now with a bucket of ice cream and a spatula crying because she can’t hold a candle to you. And who the hell wants Mr. Charlie but her. I wonder how they have sex. Bet he has to use a crane to get one of her legs up.”

“Oh, my gawd!" Piper laughed uncontrollably.

They both rounded the corner of the corn maze still laughing about Ruby Brewer when they ran straight into Charlie.

“Mr. Charlie!” Jamie Lynn gasped instinctively placing a hand over her pregnant belly.

“Good evening ladies” Charlie greeted. His voice eerily calm as he stared daggers into both their eyes.

“We were just... we were just talking about you.” Jamie Lynn cleared her throat.

“I’m sure” Charlie nodded. “I'm glad my wife’s condition amuses you two.”

“No, it’s not like that Mr. Charlie... We were just-” Piper tried to explain but Charlie wasn't hearing it.

“Good day ladies” he stalked off obviously upset.

"We don' pissed Mr. Charlie off!" Jamie Lynn shrugged as her and Piper continued to laugh. "Uh-oh Mr. Charlie the BBQ Slayer is going to get you Piper."

Eighteen

Since the last encounter with Charlie things seemed quiet for awhile. Every now and again Piper would see him sitting in the pulpit but for the most part he would have his eyes glued to his Bible and not paying any attention to her. Maybe he had finally gotten the hint.

Jamie Lynn was right, the rumors about Piper had been started by Ruby Brewer. Once her mother Pearl heard the rumors she decided to put an end to them once and for all. One call to Ruby threatening to beat her until she was skinny had put a stop to them temporarily.

For the moment things seemed peaceful. One holiday lead to the next; LJ and Phoebe seemed to sprout suddenly. Jamie Lynn had given birth to her ninth child; a bouncing baby girl she named Callie. Jamie Lynn swore on a stack of Bibles that Callie would be her last child, but Piper wasn't so sure about that.

Deputy Williams and Piper had finally made it official. By Christmas Eve everyone was gathered at Pearl's house for dinner. The house was full of chatter and intoxicating smells. A few of Piper's distant relatives drove in from Alabama to enjoy the holiday with Piper and her family. Pearl invited Jamie Lynn, Josh and their small army of kids. She also invited Deputy Williams and his parents.

"So Piper, Yance tells me you two are really serious." Mrs. Williams smiled at her from across the table.

Piper, briefly taken off guard looked at Deputy Williams with wide eyes before swallowing down her food. "I guess you can say that." She replied hesitantly. "We have gotten close these last few months. I'm trying to take things slowly, but he keeps wearing me down."

"I almost got her where I want her." Deputy Williams joked winking his eye at Piper.

"I for one hope they hurry this up." Pearl placed her napkin down on the table. "A June wedding would be nice, and I would like at least one more grand baby before I get too old."

"Mama!" Piper huffed embarrassed.

"So much for that two-kid limit." Jamie Lynn added.

Piper made faces at her mom while everyone continued to laugh at her expense. These were the moments she was missing in her life. Suddenly her phone buzzed. She lifted from the table and frowned at the screen.

"What's wrong baby?" Deputy Williams asked noticing the strange look on Piper's face.

"I just got this notification on my phone. The house alarm has been engaged."

"Should we go check it out?"

Suddenly the alarm notification switched back to SECURE. "No it appears to be nothing. Probably just a glitch in the system."

"That happens a lot this time of year." Jamie Lynn spoke up. "An animal looking for a warm place to stay for the winter may very well try to gain entry into your home. Josh you remember we came home, and that black bear was trying to get into Josh Jr's window."

"Sure do" Josh Sr. chimed in. "A couple of buckshot's to the ass and that bear was out of there in a hurry."

Piper sighed a little relieved. "Well whatever it is. Let's just hope it leaves before we get home."

###

Charlie released a slew of curse words as he struggled to get his pudgy body through the back window. The weight of his body caused his belly to scrape against the metal frame of the window.

"Argh!" Charlie let out a howl as he fell into the house. Quickly getting up to access the damage, he noticed he had torn his skin but didn't have a chance to nurse his wounds because of the beeping home alarm. He rushed down the hallway and punched in the six-digit code shutting the alarm off.

"How she gone change the locks in my damn house?" Charlie huffed aloud catching his breath. "Then she has the nerve to install an alarm system? Is she crazy?"

Thank goodness for Charlie that Piper didn't have the sense God gave her not to make the pass code her own birthday.

With the alarm system shut off Charlie casually made his way through Piper's home. A Christmas tree was lit up brightly with red and green lights; lots of presents were crowded underneath. Charlie retrieved the gift he had bought for Piper from his pocket and placed it under the tree. Then he stood back and inhaled the scent of pine as he imagined how happy she was going to be when she opened his gift.

Piper’s home was its usual messiness; dirty dishes in the sink, clean clothes left unfolded, and toys not put away. Ugh! Things would definitely have to change once he became Piper’s husband. That was for damn sure. But there was at least one bright spot to Piper’s untidy home; her dirty clothes hamper.

Smiling wickedly Charlie made his way into Piper’s master bedroom. Locating her dirty clothes hamper, he quickly rummaged through Piper’s laundry until he found what he was looking for.

A pair of red silk lace panties beckoned him. His heart pounded as he took the mesmerizing panties into his hands and inhaled Piper’s scent. He opened them up and licked the seat of them, tasting Piper’s essence. She tasted so good. He couldn't wait to taste her for real. He put the panties in his pocket and was about to look for more when a set of headlights bounced off the bedroom wall.

“Oh shit!” Charlie panicked. He rushed to the window but quickly decided he couldn’t make it out without injuring himself again. He had to hide. But where? The linen closet was cluttered. Kids closet; cluttered! Under the beds; cluttered!

“Shit! Shit! Shit!” Charlie was in a panic as the lock on the deadbolt twisted. He finally settled on Piper’s walk-in closet just in time.

Piper and Deputy Williams were engaged in a passionate kiss as they entered the house. Piper felt a gust of wind hit her shoulder and pulled away from the lip lock.

“Did you leave the window open?” she asked noticing the crack window.

Deputy Williams followed her eyes to the open window. “I’m not sure I may have.” he replied. “My bad.”

“Yance!” Piper chastised “You have to remember to secure the house. I keep telling you that!”

“I said my bad, Baby.” Yance pulled Piper into his embrace feeling the effects of the spiked eggnog he drank. “What more do you want me to say.”

“I don’t want you to *say* anything.” Piper pouted. “I just want you to be careful. That’s all.”

“I will Baby.”

“You promise?”

“I promise.” The two shared in a passionate kiss.

“We really need to wrap these gifts, Yance.” Piper moaned as Deputy Williams planted sensual kisses all over her neck and lead her to the bedroom.

“We got all night for that.”

“I’m serious Yance.” Piper walked over to her closet door to retrieve the toys she had hidden from the kids since Black Friday. She couldn't wait to see the look on the kids faces when they both unwrapped their mini iPads. She opened the closet door and Deputy Williams quickly closed it making Charlie sigh with relief. The lust in his eyes made Piper nervous as he gazed down at her.

“I said we got all night for that, Baby.”

“But morning will be here before you know it, and Mama says she’ll be here by nine.”

Deputy Williams gazed at his wrist. “So that means I got about seven hours to unwrap my Christmas gift.”

The corner of Piper’s lips curled into a naughty smile. "Hmmm… we'll see who's been naughty or nice." Piper teased removing the diamond hair pins from her tresses.

"Misses Santa I've been a very good boy." Yance played along swooping her up off her feet. Carrying Piper to the bed he laid her down gently.

Piper giggled as Yance serenaded her with kisses causing her body to tremble. The chemistry between them was magnetic and neither one could contain themselves. As his hands caressed her breast tenderly Piper removed the rest of the clothes she was wearing.

"Damn, Misses Santa!" Yance shrieked pleased with all of her curves.

"You like what you see?"

"I certainly do." He slowly placed a trail of wet kisses between her thighs.

"Ooh." Piper cooed arching her back as she enjoyed the pleasure Yance was giving her.

Piper had been long overdue for a man's affection and she welcomed everything he had to offer.

Holstering her legs up on his shoulders Yance began to devour her sweet center like a warm apple pie. Piper had never experienced foreplay this good before.

"Oh, my goodness Yance… yes right there!" Piper cooed gripping the satin bed sheets.

Hearing her passionate cries sent Yance into overdrive as he made love to her with his lips. Piper's eyes rolled into the back of her head. She couldn't stop her legs from shaking.

"YANCE!" Piper shouted his name as he brought her to the tip of her climax. She tried to control what was happening. Fluttering his tongue up against her clitoris broke the dam. "Uh-huh right there… I'm cum-ming!"

The two made passionate love like two beasts in the wild. Yance and Piper couldn't keep their hands off of one another. Even Piper was shocked at how spontaneous and exhilarating she felt being with him.

All the while inside the closet Charlie's blood was boiling. That should've been him rocking her world. Instead she was sleeping with the Deputy. *She lied to me! She said she wasn't looking for no man!* Tears of rage flooded down his face as he watched Deputy Williams ravage Piper.

How could she do this to me? Us? Fucking whore!

Piper was his woman. He just needed more time to make her understand that. The voices in his head taunted him. He bit down on his knuckles until he drew blood and silently sobbed rocking back and forth inside the closet until Piper and the Deputy were fast asleep. She wasn't getting away with this, it was far from over. Piper had some making up to do.

Nineteen

Piper jolted from her sleep at the wee hours of the morning. She could have sworn somebody was standing over her, watching her as she slept. Deputy Williams lay slightly snoring beside her. Unable to sleep Piper climbed out of bed and decided to go wrap the gifts she had intended to wrap before Yance got a hold of her.

Smiling to herself, she covered her naked body in a silk robe and made her way to the living room. She noticed the sliding glass door was cracked.

"Ugh! Yance!" she hissed her teeth; securing the door. She really didn't mind him sleeping over from time to time but he never made sure the home was secure.

"This is all the security I need, Baby" he would say holding up his gun. Piper shook her head; kneeling down beside the Christmas tree with a handful of unwrapped gifts.

Once she was done with all her gift wrapping she stood back and admired her handy work. Each gift was perfectly wrapped with its own color coordinated ribbon and bow. Piper was feeling proud of herself and what she was able to accomplish without the help of her kids' father or his money.

Then something caught her eye; a small Christmas gift in the shape of a rectangle. It was neatly put together with scotch tape but the wrapping didn't match any of the other gifts. P-I-P-E-R was spelled out in big block letters on a piece of Manilla tape across the front of it. Piper smiled thinking that Deputy Williams had planted the small gift there for her.

Quickly as it came Piper's smile faded and turned to shock once she read the other name written on the gift. She ripped open the box and screamed dropping the gift to the floor. "Yance! Get up Yance! He's been in my house!"

Deputy Williams came running down the hallway wearing only his boxer shorts. "What is it, Baby?"

Piper's hands trembled as she pointed at the gift from Charles Brewer. With confusion etched on his face Deputy Williams opened the gift. His jaw dropped when he discovered that inside the gift box was a note Charlie had written to Piper expressing his love and admiration for her; and along with that note was every single Money Order that Piper had sent to him for the rent… uncashed.

“Uh-huh, I gotta get outta here... I gotta get me and my kids outta here today!”

By the time Pearl showed up with the kids Piper was in her living room pacing back and forth having a panic attack. She couldn't believe how bold and crazy Charles Brewer was acting.

“What’s going on here?” Pearl asked with concern in her eyes. Deputy Williams was rubbing his hands over his head staring at Piper. “Piper what happened?”

“He’s been in my house again, Mama.”

“Who?”

“Mr. Charlie!”

“Charlie’s been in here? Why didn't you tell me girl!”

Deputy Williams tried to calm the situation down and spoke up. “She believes that Mr. Charles has been breaking in here when she and the kids are not here, but-”

“There is no “but” Yance!” Piper shouted. "He has been in here! Oh, Mama I’m so sorry that I haven't told you sooner."

"There, there child." Pearl hugged her daughter. "Keep your voice down before you scare the kids." Pearl looked up at Deputy Williams. "Well you the police… Aren't you going to do something?"

"I'll talk to him." Deputy Williams said seeing no other option.

"Please do before, I have to." Piper hissed fuming.

###

It was tradition for Charles Brewer to close-up his BBQ stand during the winter months. With all that he had going on his health problems and increased obsession with Piper Jackson he hadn't had the time to get his affairs in order.

The owners of the gas station where he usually parked his food truck were nice enough to allow him to park it in the lot behind the store during the holidays for free. That was a relief for Charlie seeing as though he didn't have to worry about paying for storage.

It was Christmas Day and the town was quiet. Most residents were inside on this cold morning opening up overpriced Christmas gifts. Charlie took this time to do his inventory and collect his receipts for the upcoming tax season. After handling his business, he secured his food truck and headed home.

On the way home, he turned on the radio. He was surprised to hear a familiar song come across the airways. *"We're talking Lights, Camera, Action!! Got me saying I'm sorry Ms. Jackson!"*

Charlie bobbed his head to the music. Charlie swore it was a sign from God that he and Piper Jackson belonged together. Charlie was so into the music that he hadn't realized he was being followed until a set of police lights started flashing behind him. Bearing a confused look on his face Charlie pulled his truck over on the side of the highway.

Deputy Williams climbed out of his police cruiser in plain clothes, walked up to Charlie's driver side window and rapped on the window twice.

Rolling down his window, Charlie put on a friendly smile. "What seems to be the problem officer."

"Step out of the car for a second Mr. Charlie I need to talk to you." Deputy Williams spoke sternly. "It's about Piper Jackson."

Charlie proceeded with caution, climbing out of his vehicle and closing the door. He leaned up against his door with his arms folded across his chest. His eyes sized up the Deputy as he tried to gauge his demeanor.

"What about Piper Jackson?" He asked.

"Well" Deputy Williams began "She has some serious concerns about you coming into her house uninvited. She says that you've been just popping-up over there unannounced."

"Shoot, that's just simply not true Deputy" Charlie swore. "I would never... you know me."

Deputy Williams nodded and retrieved Charlie's gift from his front pocket. "Care to tell me how this showed up under Piper's Christmas tree this morning then?"

Charlie eyed his gift to Piper and his heart started racing. "Oh that" he laughed nervously. "That's nothing. You see, Piper has been struggling to pay the rent for some time now. I overheard her telling one of the ladies at the church she didn't know how she would be able to pay her bills after the holidays after she got the kids Christmas gifts. I thought maybe you would be helping her out since you're always up her tail but once I saw that you're only good warming her bed I decided to step in. I hope you don't mind Deputy I was just helping you out."

His condescending talk caused Deputy Williams to clench his jaws. The law didn't make a whole lot of money in this town but he was confident that he could still be a provider. Even if he couldn't provide for Piper, he for damn sure could protect her.

Yance made a step towards Charlie and leveled his lids so that he and Charlie were eye to eye. "Mr. Charlie my parents always taught me to respect my elders. That is the only reason why I'm not going to smack the taste out your mouth for disrespecting me. Instead I'm going to offer you a warning. Back off...

or next time our encounter won't be so friendly. Have a good day now!"

Twenty

Satisfied with the conversation that he had with Mr. Charlie; Deputy Williams had tried to convince Piper that she was safe to live in the mobile home. He even offered to move in to make sure she and the kids felt safe. Piper agreed to stay there at least until her lease was up.

Just as Piper was starting to feel comfortable, the mysterious phone calls began.

"Hello?" She whispered into the phone.

Turn it around let me see something!
Telling you now it's gone be something.
We're talking lights camera action…
Got me singing I'm sorry Miss Jackson!

The loud music came blaring through the phone. Piper looked over at the clock on the nightstand. The time read 3:49 am. "Who is this?" She demanded.

The music suddenly stopped and there was a heavy breathing on the phone. Piper hung up the phone only for the phone to ring again a minute later. The mysterious caller continued with the excessive calls in the middle of the night; the same song playing along with heavy breathing.

Then one-night Piper heard his voice. The breathing was extra heavy this time and rhythmic; like a man reaching a climax.

"Who is this? Why do you keep calling me?"

There was a pause, then more heavy breathing. "Uh, I love you" the voice finally bellowed out in a whisper.

"Mr. Charlie?" Piper gasped; her eyes widened with shock. "Mr. Charlie? What the hell-"

The caller quickly ended the call and the line went dead. Piper sat up in bed feeling confused and disgusted. Why would this deranged fool call her and masturbate over the phone? Piper had no idea what type of monster she was dealing with? Soon… very soon she would find out.

The winter had come and gone, and the snow had finally melted. The bleak skies were now brighter with rays of sunshine casting down over the small town. It was the Friday before the kid's spring break and Deputy Williams was planning to take Piper and the kids to Orlando, Florida to spend the week at Disney World.

Piper was supposed to get off work at three that afternoon but it seemed like everyone and their mother had an issue that needed medical attention. She tried letting Deputy Williams know that she was running behind schedule but every call was sent straight to his voice mail. Running late, Piper was speeding towards the kids' school when her phone rang. "Hello?"

"Hello Ms. Jackson, Lee Brown here." Piper's attorney's voice filled the cabin of her SUV.

"Lee!" Piper greeted excitedly. "Please tell me you have some good news for me."

"I got some good news for you!" Lee beamed. "I've found a buyer for your property."

"Yes!"

"And they are willing to pay the asking price."

"That is just awesome!" Piper said as she pulled up to the crowded pick up line at the school. She watched children filing into the cars ahead of hers as she got the particulars "So how soon can we close?"

"How does the end of next month sound to you?"

“Perfect!” Piper shouted. That would put her closing date sometime at the end of April.

She could use the money to go look for her and the kids a new place. Piper was even thinking she would ask Deputy Williams to move with them. Piper was so busy celebrating she hadn’t even noticed her children had yet to make it to the car. Usually LJ was so anxious to get home to play his silly video games, he would be dragging his little sister by her hot-pink backpack as soon as he saw Piper.

Piper made it to the front of the line and scanned the curb. No kids! She spotted L.J’s teacher near the entrance and rolled down her window. “Excuse me, Ms. Nimitz?” she smiled at the friendly faced teacher. “I’m here to pick up my children. I know I’m late.”

“Oh…” Ms. Nimitz offered Piper an unsure smile. “The children were picked up a half hour ago.”

“Really?” Piper frowned. She quickly realized that Deputy Williams must’ve heard one of her messages and decided to pick up the kids himself. That was fine but she just wished he would have notified her first. “Okay thanks” she said driving off. Once back on the road Piper hit up Deputy Williams on speed dial.

“What’s up Sexy?” His smooth voice greeted

her ears causing her to smile.

"You're finally answering your phone?"

"Sorry no reception way out here in the sticks." Deputy Williams laughed "What's good with you? You ready to go see Mickey and them?"

"I'm ready for a vacation. That's for damn sure." Piper harrumphed.

"I heard that. I'll be at the house in about thirty minutes and we can get this party started."

"Sounds good... And since you were nice enough to pick up the kids I'll pick up dinner."

"The kids?"

"Yeah you could've told me you were going to pick them up. It sure would've saved me a trip to the-"

"Piper?"

"Yeah"

"I don't have the kids..."

"Boy stop playing. I already know you picked them up a half hour ago. Now what you want for dinner?"

“Piper! Listen to me! I don’t have the kids!”

The seriousness in his voice gave Piper pause. The hairs on the back of her neck stood up at attention. “What?”

“I don't have the kids!” he repeated.

“Oh my God!”

“Where are you now?”

“I’m just leaving the school and was headed to the house… Lord please don’t let nothing happen to my babies!”

“Baby don’t panic.” Deputy Williams tried to soothe her to no avail. “Maybe Ms. Pearl picked them up. Just go to the house and wait for me there. Okay?”

“Okay” Piper’s eyes welled up with tears as she pressed down on the accelerator. Moments later Piper pulled up to her home.

The sight of Charles Brewer’s old truck caused her heart to fall at her feet. Then she felt a certain anger began to bubble up so bad steam was coming out of her head. Piper was seeing red when she walked into her home to see Charlie seated at the table feeding her daughter ice cream.

“Look Mama Mr. Charlie bought us ice cream.” L.J. presented Piper with a halfway melted ice cream cone with sprinkles on top.

“Kids go to your room.” Piper ordered through clenched teeth never taking her eyes off of Charlie.

The kids sensing the tension in their mother’s voice took heed and did as they were told, but not before giving Mr. Charlie a hard time.

“Ooh Mr. Charlie you're in big trouble.” Phoebe May sang before scurrying off to her room.

Seeing the coast was clear Piper lost her cool. “You must be outside your rabbit ass mind.” Piper growled.

“Wait Darling I know you’re upset. Let me explain.”

“YOU TOOK MY KIDS!!!” Piper screamed. “What part of your deranged mind would make you think that this is okay?”

“I was just trying to help. I’m sorry.” Mr. Charlie apologized. “I know how hard you work. I was riding by the kids school and just thought if I picked them up for you-”

"Why are you riding past their school? Why are you still coming around after Yance has already asked you to back off? What is wrong with you?"

"I'm sorry." Charlie murmured.

Piper stood there with her chest heaving. Her head was pounding, her heart was racing; her whole body shook with anger. All things had come to a head in this moment. Up until now Piper had tried to be civil. She had tried to be reasonable with Charlie. Piper even tried to be understanding of his P.T.S.D. and his mood swings.

Not to mention the talk she had to make Charlie understand that she only wanted to be friends with him in the nicest way possible. But, Charlie wasn't trying to comprehend anything. He didn't give a damn about what Piper wanted. He still pursued her despite her efforts to curb his advances. He had crossed every single boundary she had set up.

Now he had completely crossed the line by taking her precious children. There was no turning back or enough apologies. She was done being patient. Piper was done being nice.

"If you come near me or my children again, I will have you arrested." Piper spoke firmly. "Do you understand me?"

“I understand, Darling” Charlie appeared to hang his head in shame. “I understand… that you ain’t nothing but an ol’ ungrateful ass bitch!”

The sudden shift in Charlie’s demeanor startled Piper. She backed up against the kitchen counter as Charlie made looming steps towards her. “I-I welcomed you” he spoke with conviction. “I gave you food. I helped you get a job. I gave you a good place to live and didn’t charge you a dime in rent. Who else gonna let you live rent free?”

“What are you talking about?” Piper was confused. “Mr. Charlie I paid my rent.”

“I gave it back to you, Bitch!” Charlie snapped then tried to regain his composure. “I gave you the rent money back because I don’t want any money from you, Darling. I- I just want you to appreciate me and allow me to take care of you. Please, just let me show you how a man is supposed to treat a woman.

Piper’s head cocked to one side. She couldn’t believe her ears “HELL NO! Mr. Charlie that is never going to happen! What part of that don’t you get!"

Charlie’s jaws tightened and his nostrils flared. “So you would rather spread your legs and give your dead coochie to a negro that can’t afford to give you nothing!" He growled; spittle flying from his mouth. "Y'all living in my house! Deputy Williams can't even provide you with a place to lay your head and you would choose him over me?"

"Get out!" Piper gritted pointing towards the door.

Charlie let out a sinister chuckle. "This is my house. I'll leave when I get good and gawd damn ready. Why don't you leave? Yeah, why don't you and your bad ass kids just go back to ya' mammy house. You can keep her place nasty like you do mine. You raggedy bitch! No wonder your life's in shambles. Your priorities are all fucked up! It's your fault your kids ain't got no home training. Now I see why your ex husband became a faggot!"

WHAP!!! Piper's hand trembled after it collided with Charlie's cheek, knocking his glasses to the floor. A flash of anger came to Charlie's eyes but quickly dissipated when he noticed the knife Piper had swiped from the butcher block.

"Don't you ever disrespect me like that in your life! Who do you think you are? You don't know anything about me. What you need to know is that I don't want YOU! Yance will be here any moment. Get the hell out!" She warned him with the knife aimed at him. "Leave!"

Charlie calmly ran his tongue along the metallic tasting blood on his bottom lip. “You just made a huge mistake, Darling.” He grimaced. “Now I’m going to have to do you like I used to do my new recruits back in the army. I’m going to build you up… by breaking you all the way down.”

Twenty-One

*I*nside the sanctuary of the church Johnnie Mae Williams wore a mask of frustration. As the director of the church's praise team it was her responsibility to get the praise dancers on one accord before the annual spring festival. The festival was in two days and nobody but Johnnie Mae seemed to know what they were doing. The two white girls were dancing offbeat and one of the healthy built praise dancers had just split the center of her leotard.

"Stop! Just stop!" Johnnie Mae waved her hands in the air. She punched the pause button on the boombox and looked at her flock in bewilderment. "What are y'all doing? Do y'all even want to be here?"

"Yes ma'am!" They all replied in unison.

"Well y'all had better get it together." Johnnie Mae demanded. "Becky and Megan get with Shalonda and Dricka so they can show y'all how to move on beat. And Jackie baby you know your butt is bigger than a STOP sign, please tell your mama she needs to buy you a costume that fits you."

"Yes ma'am" Jackie mumbled hanging her head in shame.

"We only got two days to get it together ladies." Johnnie Mae warned "How y'all think Pastor gone feel with all these important dignitaries here and y'all up here on stage looking a mess? Huh?"

Before anyone had a chance to speak the doors to the church sanctuary opened. At first Johnnie Mae could hardly make out the dark figure entering in the church. But then Charles Brewer came into view and the whole church went silent.

"Charlie? Is that you? Oh my God is that blood on your shirt?"

Charlie stumbled into the church with blood on his shirt. His lips were swollen and bloody and both of his eyes were black.

"Call an ambulance!" He huffed before collapsing on a church pew. "I've been attacked."

“Who attacked you?” Johnnie Mae asked frightened.

“It was Piper… Piper Jackson!”

###

The following Sunday was the day of the Spring Festival. Pearl Crosby had stayed up all night sewing the angel costumes that L.J. and Phoebe would be wearing to sing in the children’s choir. The church was packed and Piper was excited to see her babies perform in front of the congregations of neighboring churches. Her excitement was short lived however the minute she stepped foot inside the sanctuary.

Piper tried her best to ignore the dirty looks and quiet whispers as she sat down next to Deputy Williams in one of the church pews. As leader of the women’s usher board Pearl stood on the side of pulpit. Her eyes were glued to Piper and she could sense that something in the air wasn’t right. Charles Brewer’s Deacon seat sat empty and that was totally out of character for him seeing as though he had never missed a Spring Festival.

Reverend Snowden, a pastor from nearby

Mayville, Georgia was the guest speaker for the day. He took his place at the podium looking like a 1970's pimp with his freshly relaxed hair finger waved to the back and a large gold crossed dangling from his robe. He peered out into the crowd and locked eyes on Piper.

"Let the church say amen." He droned.

"Amen!" the congregation shouted back.

"For those of you who do not know who I am. My name is Reverend Snowden. I am from the Mayville Church of God in Christ in Mayville, Georgia. We are a small church but the spirit of the Lord dwells within, Amen?"

"Amen!" the congregation shouted back.

"Brothers and Sisters my heart is sad and heavy laden this morning. It has come to my attention that Deacon Brewer won't be in attendance with us today. It seems that he is in the hospital suffering from a vicious attack."

There was a noticeable gasp that escaped the audience. Johnnie Mae Williams shot daggers at Piper over her shoulder. Piper shifted uncomfortably in her seat unsure of where Reverend Snowden was going with his sermon.

“I have known Deacon Brewer for at least twenty years now.” Reverend Snowden continued. “I know that he is a good man; a good Deacon. The type of man that will offer you the shirt off his back; a true man of God!”

“Yes!” the crowd shouted.

“What a shame that someone would attack such a man!”

“A shame and a scandal!” one lady shouted. “A shame and a scandal!”

“Brother’s and Sister’s today was supposed to be a day of celebration” Reverend Snowden preached. “It was supposed to be a day that with celebrate a time of rebirth! But unfortunately today we must remind ourselves of the wickedness in our mist. Please turn your Bible’s to First Kings. Verse seventeen begins the story of Jezebel. She was the wife of Ahab the king of Israel. The Bible says that Jezebel was a wicked woman who used her beauty to manipulate men. She preyed on both her husband and other people’s husband’s as well. Do y’all hear what I’m saying to y’all?”

“Yes Rev.!” they all screamed.

“There is a Jezebel right here in our mist!”

"Yes!"

"She is a liar!"

"Yes!

"A manipulator!"

"Yes!"

"A deceiver!"

"Yes!" The congregation shoutcd in unison.

"And a homewrecker!"

"Yes!"

"We must do like Jehu and expose this Jezebel! We must throw this Jezebel out of the window and allow the dogs to eat her up before her wickedness can consume us all!"

Johnnie Mae, moved by the spirit suddenly jumped to her feet and shouted. "There she is, Reverend!" she pointed a sharp finger at Piper. "There's the Jezebel who attacked the Good Deacon!"

Piper was mortified as the whole congregation turned against her. People she had known since she was a child all standing around chanting. “Jezebel”

Unable to control her tears and embarrassment she ran out of the church with Deputy Williams fast on her heels. Pearl Crosby was so filled with anger that these people she called her friends would try to shame Piper in front of her own children it made her sick to her stomach.

“Lies!” she screamed with so much conviction that it quieted the crowd. She was sure that this would be the last time she stepped foot in this God forsaken church and she intended to let the people know what she truly felt about them.

“Look at ya!” she snarled. “All of you ought to be ashamed of yourselves; calling yourselves people of God. You all sit around here on your high horses looking down on my child because of Charles Brewer? He gives you his money and makes sure your fat butts stay full of his pork sandwiches and you ready to believe everything he says as law. Well I’m here to tell ya' that Charlie is not Godly by any means. He is a monster and you all will find out soon enough!”

“Sister Pearl…” Johnnie Mae reached for Pearl’s arm.

“Getcho got damn hands off me!” Pearl glared at Johnnie Mae. “You want to call my daughter a

Jezebel like your pussy ain't got no miles on it. Tell your husband how I caught you and Deacon Sims humping in the fellowship hall during fall festival two years ago." The crowd gasped.

"She's lying!" Johnnie Mae denied while Deacon Sims tried to cover his reddened face.

"None of you are saints!" Pearl continued. "Just a bunch of sinners who don't have a heaven, a hell, or a jail cell to put my baby in so you can all just go straight to hell!"

The congregation watched in shock as Pearl gathered up her grand children and left the church for good.

###

"Who's ready for Disney World?" Deputy Williams bounced to the kitchen table wearing a Mickey Mouse shirt and some mouse ears.

"Me!" The kids hollered in unison.

Deputy Williams noticed that Piper looked sad as she picked over her pancakes.

"Come on babe, get excited." Deputy Williams pleaded placing a pair of mouse ears on Piper's head.

“I'm trying.” Piper forced a smile.

Deputy Williams took her by the hand and guided her into the living room away from the children.

“Today is a new day. I already got the report filed and Charlie should be served Monday morning.” Deputy Williams assured her. “I promise we will deal with Charlie soon enough. But, let’s not allow him or those stupid people at the church to ruin our vacation... please.”

“Ok” Piper smiled and allowed Deputy Williams to kiss her on the lips.

Suddenly the doorbell rang. “I’ll get that. You get the kids cleaned up so we can hit the highway.” Deputy Williams playfully smacked Piper on her backside before bopping up to the front door.

His smile faded when he noticed two uniformed officers standing on the other side. “Hank? Tina? What y’all doing here?” Deputy Williams asked in confusion.

“Is Piper Jackson home?” Tina asked disregarding Deputy Williams.

“Um...Yes.” Deputy Williams replied cautiously. “Piper! Piper come here Baby!”

Deputy Williams returned his attention to the officers "What's this about?"

From inside the kitchen Piper could hear walkie talkie's squawking. When she rounded the corner she was surprised to see the police standing at her door. "What's going on?"

"Hello Ms. Jackson" the male officer greeted her. "I'm officer Hank Brown and this is officer Tina Adams. We're here on a matter regarding Charles Brewer. Do you recall the last encounter you had with him?"

"Yes...he came here on Friday...I asked him to leave."

"Well ma'am Charles Brewer has sustained multiple injuries to his face and he says you assaulted him." Officer Tina spoke up.

"I didn't assault him!" Piper defended. She looked to Deputy Williams for help.

"There must be some misunderstanding." Deputy Williams spat. "Piper didn't assault him."

"I didn't assault him he's lying." Piper repeated herself.

"Yance, he's claiming she struck him several

times in the face." Officer Hank said.

"We heard there have been some speculations going on around town but Piper never touched him." Deputy Williams looked at Piper. "Right Baby?"

"No!" Piper hissed obviously upset. "I mean I slapped him once but-"

"You slapped him?" Deputy Williams grilled her surprised.

"He had taken my kids. He wouldn't leave my house! He was threatening me!"

"So you slapped him?" Officer Tina reiterated. "Ma'am that's assault. Now I'm afraid I need to ask you to turn around and put your hands behind your back. You're being arrested for abuse of the elderly."

Twenty-Three

Piper couldn't believe what was happening to her. She was so close to getting her life all the way back on track. Now she was sitting in a small mildew smelling court room facing a year in jail for a crime she didn't commit.

Perplexed as she watched on in horror as Charles Brewer took the stand. Covered in bruises and bandages he described to the judge how Piper had savagely beat him because he refused to sleep with her.

"It's true your honor." Ruby Brewer piped in. "She even tried to jump on me at the hospital when my dear husband was in there fighting for his life."

In the end Piper was sentenced to a year of probation, one hundred hours of community service, and ordered to stay one thousand feet away from Charlie at all times. The judge had denied her complaint against Charlie for harassment. Piper found out quickly that not just the church but the whole town was against her. Charles Brewer had the entire town of Conners thinking that he was a saint and she was a sinner.

As soon as Piper was let out of jail, she found an eviction notice taped to her front door. She had thirty days to vacate the premises due to nonpayment of the rent. On top of that someone had flattened all four of the tires on her SUV and Department of Children and Families showed up to remove Piper's kids based on an anonymous call of child abuse.

Piper was sure it was Charlie but with all the hate she got from the town's folks she couldn't be so sure. The law was certainly on Charlie's side and he was free to wreak havoc on Piper and that is exactly what he did.

The harassing phone calls started back up a week after court and this time Charlie didn't even bother to try and hide his identity.

"Hello?" Piper spoke groggily into the phone at four o'clock in the morning.

"Well hello there, Darling." Charlie's creepy voice spoke through the receiver.

"How did you get this number?"

"I have my ways, Darling." Charlie laughed. "I don't know why you keep changing your phone number. You can't escape me!" Charlie chuckled sinisterly.

“Go to hell!” Piper hung up the phone only for the phone to ring again. Piper sat straight up in bed. “Stop contacting me!”

“Relax Darling no need to fret.” Charlie laughed. “I know you mad at me but I just wanted you to know I’m cooking a new flavor of ribs today. Got the fat back in the collard greens just like you like it. Extra cheesy macaroni too. Why don't you come through and get you a plate today.”

“Leave me the hell alone!” Piper screamed hanging up the phone. The phone continued to ring excessively until Piper answered it again.

“Don’t you hang up on me again ya’ raggedy bitch! I’ll leave your ass stanking bad somewhere! I’ll make you disappear, bitch! I swear to gawd!”

She blocked his number only for him to call from a new line. Piper got her number changed a week later and Charlie simply called his friends at the phone company to get her new number. He called at all hours of the day and night. He could be nice or nasty depending on his mood or how much liquor he had to drink. Sometimes he would invite her to lunch. Other times he would invite her to come sit on his face.

After weeks of continuous harassment Piper finally had enough and went to the police station.

“This is ridiculous! Aren’t you going to do anything about this?” Piper pleaded with the police.

The lazy clerk behind the desk at the police station looked at Piper with dead pan eyes. “Has Charles Brewer harmed you physically?”

“Well no but-”

“Sorry Ma’am there’s nothing we can do.”

“But I have his voice recorded. You haven’t even asked to hear it. He’s threatening to kill me!”

“Ma’am there is nothing we can do.”

Piper was defeated. All her cries for help were falling on deaf ears.

“It’s going to be okay Baby” Deputy Williams hugged her. He looked at his co-workers. “I can’t believe y’all doing her like this.”

“Maybe she would be happier if she went back to where she came from.” One of the clerk's spat giving Piper a nasty look.

“Who in the hell do you think you are talking too?” Piper was ready for a fight before Deputy Williams stopped her. She yanked away from him and headed out the door.

“We will find another way, Babe.” he promised. “Don’t let them get to you.”

“How?” Piper turned her frustration out on Deputy Williams. “How? How are we going to find another way, Yance? The man is stalking me, harassing me, hell the bastard even took my kid’s, and nothing is being done about it. If there was another way we need to use it now! So whatchu got? I'm listening.”

After Deputy Williams failed to producc the words that would make Piper feel better about the situation she turned to walk away.

“I gotta go... I’m going to be late for work.” she droned before getting into her car.

Piper immediately felt bad for going off on Yance like she did. He was only trying to help. It wasn’t his fault Charlie was crazily obsessed. Piper picked up her cell phone and tried to dial his number but it went straight to voicemail. She figured she would give him some space and call him back later.

Luckily for Piper she had work to take her mind off her situation. High School sports were big in a small town like Conners. So much so the school board decided to spread the physicals into different parts of the year. Soon the tiny clinic on Main Street was wall to wall with gargantuan sized teenagers waiting to see if they were going to be physically fit to play in the summer football games.

Piper was moving a mile a minute back and forth between patient exam rooms. By noon she had taken so many blood pressures and filled out so many questionnaires her head was about to explode.

Deciding to take a break sitting at her desk she rubbed her temples to erase the tiredness. Then suddenly the phone rang.

"Conners Clinic… Piper speaking... How may I help you today?"

Uh shorty, turn it around lemme see somethin...

Messin with me for real, it's gone be somethin…

Yea, I'm talking Lights, Camera, Action! Have me singin', I'm sorry Miss Jackson...

"Listen Darling, their playing our song." Charlie beamed as the familiar song haunted Piper.

"What do you want Charlie?"

"I saw you up at the police station this

morning. I keep trying to tell you that you can't escape me, Piper. I got this whole town eating out the palm of my hand. No one will ever believe you no matter what you say. Now if you're a good girl and learn your place, I might lift that restraining order. What do you think of that?"

"I think you should roll over and die! You will never have me!"

"Well suit yourself you ungrateful bitch. Say goodbye to your job."

Charlie hung up the phone in Piper's face leaving her confused. *What did he mean by say goodbye to my job?*

Just then Jamie Lynn came rushing in with a worrisome look on her face. "Piper you ain't gone believe this, Hunny." She said shoving a shiny flyer in Pipers face.

Piper squinted her eyes as she read the words printed on the flyer. "Charlie's BBQ… Grand reopening! New location… North Main Street?" A wave of shock splashed over Piper as she realized what Charlie had said to her.

"What are you doing? Wait Piper you're not going out there are you? What about…What about the restraining order, Sugar?!"

Piper was already out the door before Jamie Lynn could finish her plea. The building across the street had sat vacant just the previous Friday. Now it was Monday and the line was wrapped around the block.

A giant Charlie's BBQ sign with a fat pink pig advertised free rib sandwiches for the whole town to see. Charlie seemed happy as clam passing out his free rib sandwiches to the eager customers. He casted his bespectacled eyes at Piper glaring at him from across the street. The smug look on his face was enough to bring hot angry tears to Piper's eyes.

"He's trying to break me" Piper spoke in a low voice. "First with the church; then with my children, then with my home. Now he's taken my livelihood away from me too."

"Your livelihood?" Jamie Lynn looked confused. "Piper what are you saying?"

"How far would you say his restaurant is from your clinic?"

"I don't know" Jamie Lynn shrugged. "Maybe eight hundred feet, I guess."

"The law says that I have to stay one thousand feet away from Charlie at all times. So that means I can't work here."

"Oh, my goodness, Piper I'm so sorry." Jamie Lynn placed her hand over her mouth. "We can fight this."

Just then the old red station wagon drove pass. Piper locked eyes with the driver. An idea popped into her head. "You're damn right we're going to fight this." Piper stormed back into the clinic with Jamie Lynn hot on her heels.

"What are you going to do?" Jamie Lynn inquired.

Piper made it to her desk and turned her purse upside down. Dumping out all its contents, she rummaged through the papers until she found what she was looking for. She quickly picked up the phone and dialed Deputy Williams' number hoping he would pick up.

"Baby, I'm so sorry" Deputy Williams answered the phone on the first ring.

"Me too." Piper said "Listen I need you to write this down. O-G-V-8-3-6. It's a licensed plate number to a station wagon. I believe the owner of that station wagon can help us.

Twenty-Four

Welcome to Mayville, Georgia the sign read as Piper's SUV crossed the county line into the small farming town. Piper made a right turn at a dirt road following the path all the way up to a cow pasture. To the left of the pasture sat a small house; white in color with periwinkle blue shutters and doors.

Piper quickly recognized the red station wagon parked on the carport and pulled up behind it. The quietness in the air caused Piper's heart to race a bit. She walked up to the front door and knocked. No answer. She knocked again. Still no answer. There was a window off to the side of the door. Figuring somebody had to be home she decided to peek inside.

"What are you doing here?" A voice suddenly startled Piper. She spun around clutching her chest.

Margaret Robinson offered a distrustful gaze as she stood before Piper wearing a lime green gardening hat and polka dot gardening gloves. A small pair of pruning shears was clutched in one of her hands.

Piper sucked in a breath. “Mrs. Robinson my name is-”

“I know who you are.” Margaret interrupted Piper. “What do you want?”

“Well I was hoping you could give me some information on Charles Brewer. I understand you had a daughter who was once his tenant. Charlie told me she committed suicide but I don’t believe him. I fear the same thing he’s doing to me… he did to her.”

There was a long pause as Margaret took her time sizing Piper up. Finally she let out a sigh. “Come on” she mumbled.

Piper followed Margaret through a side entrance leading to a washroom where Margaret removed her gloves and kicked off her shoes. Then the two entered the Robinson home which was a complete hoarded mess. Newspapers were piled as high as the ceiling. Milk crates containing random objects were stacked, one on top of the other, gathering dust in the corner of the living room. Aluminum cans and discarded glass bottles seem to have never made it to the recycler as they rested in a sea of garbage bags in the kitchen.

“Excuse the mess” Margaret said while clearing a place for Piper to sit on the couch in the living room. “I wasn’t expecting company.”

Piper nodded her head as she quietly sat and took in the chaotic scene around her. The only other clean spot was a faded blue reclining chair parked in front of the television. Next to the chair sat an old oxygen tank and a bedside commode with the name E-A-R-L- R-O-B-I-N-S-O-N spelled out in block letters with a sharpie.

On the fireplace mantle Earl Robinson’s funeral program sat on display next to a vase of wilted flowers and other family pictures. Margaret walked over to the mantle and lifted one of the framed pictures leaving a trail of dust behind.

“This was my daughter, Teresa” Margaret informed gently placing the frame in Piper’s hand.

Piper deduced that the picture of Teresa must’ve been taken back in the late 90’s or early 2000’s judging by the wet and wavy weave she wore. Aside from her eyebrows being drawn on and the hideous black lip liner on her lips Teresa Robinson was beautiful.

“This is how I want to remember my baby.” Margaret smiled weakly. “She looked beautiful when the sparkle was still in her eyes.”

"She was very pretty." Piper handed Margaret back the frame. "What happened to her?"

"Drugs!" Margaret spat angrily. "She got in with the wrong crowd in her teenage years and had been on a downward spiral ever since."

"I'm sorry to hear that."

"Don't be because God is able, and he delivered my baby from her addictions. Teresa was doing well for herself. She had her whole life ahcad of her... Then she met Charles Brewer and all that changed."

Hearing Charlie's name made Piper shiver with both anger and fear, "I'm afraid to ask what he did to her."

"Same thing he done to you." Margaret replied. "Call himself helping Teresa out. Offered her money, helped her find a job, gave her a place to stay. In fact, she was murdered in the same trailer you are living in now."

The revelation caused Piper to shift uncomfortably in her seat. She cleared her throat.

"Charlie said she swallowed a bunch of pills and killed herself."

“Charlie’s a damn lie!” Margaret quipped. “My baby was a drug addict but she ain’t wanna kill herself. Teresa was too trusting of people and Charlie took advantage of that. She allowed him into her home and he tried to rape her. Luckily, she was able to fight him off but when she went to the police to press charges nobody believed her. She was just a lowlife crackhead and he was the Good Deacon. The whole town of Conners turned on Teresa.”

“I know the feeling.” Piper mumbled under her breath.

“Charles Brewer is the devil.” Margaret spat bitterly. “But I promise I will go to my grave fighting for justice.”

Piper noticed the seriousness in Margaret’s eyes. “I want to help you fight for justice that's why I’m here, Mrs. Robinson. Charlie has taken everything away from me and I won't allow him to get away with it. My lawyer, Lee Brown out of Atlanta is tight with a few detectives on the Atlanta Police Department. They can help us but they are going to need leads. Is there anything Teresa told you before she died? Anything that will help us get the investigation started?”

Margaret pondered for a moment. “There is one incident that stood out to me. Teresa said Charlie had started watching her every move. Somehow, he knew what time she went to bed at night and what time she woke up in the mornings. He would call her to wish her a good morning every morning and her phone would ring as soon as she stepped foot inside her door in the evening. One night Teresa decided to go to the Tavern with a couple of her co-workers after work. She got home later than usual and Charlie called her in a fit of rage. He called her a whore and demanded to know who she had been out screwing. That's when he threatened to kill her. He said he had killed before and he would do it again. Teresa was dead a week later."

"Oh my God!" Piper gasped.

Margaret continued with the story. "Charlie said he had killed before. So after Teresa was murdered I decided to do some digging. Let me show you what I found." Margaret disappeared and returned a moment later holding a newspaper clipping.

The headline read: ARMY CADET BODY FOUND SLAIN ON ARMY BASE. Underneath was a picture of a young woman dressed in an Army uniform.

"Her name was Erica Jenkins" Margaret informed. "She was found dead in a dumpster three weeks into her basic training."

"It says here that no suspects were ever found." Piper replied.

"Yeah but look at who they say discovered the body."

Piper read aloud. "The body of Ms. Jenkins was found on July 9th at 4:53am by… Sergeant Major Charles Brewer."

Piper hands began to tremble as she imagined the terror Erica Jenkins must have felt during her final moments of life.

"It's no coincidence that the man who discovers the body of a young nineteen-year old girl would be the same man who terrorizes other young women." Margaret shook her head, "I'm not sure about a lot of things Ms. Piper but I'm sure Charlie is a murderer and I aim to prove it. That's why I've been sneaking around Conners. I'm watching Charlie like he watched my daughter. Keep waiting for him to make a mistake. Charlie is a slick devil, but this fight isn't over. My husband died of a broken heart and on his deathbed, I promised I would get justice for our baby girl."

Piper stood to her feet. "And together we will keep that promise Mrs. Robinson. Do you mind if I take these newspaper clippings with me? I'm sure an investigation into this young lady's murder will shed light on Teresa's case and finally bring Charles Brewer to justice."

"Take whatever you need, Baby." Margaret tittered. "The sooner we drive the nails in that devil's coffin the better."

Twenty-Five

Beyond motivated to get Charles Brewer a dose of his own medicine Piper was more than determined after speaking with Margaret to bring Mr. Charlie down. The investigators informed her that they indeed began looking into the Erica Jenkins case.

Piper was sure it was only a matter of time before Mr. Charlie would be exposed for the monster that he was. DCFS had finally deemed Piper a fit mother and returned her kids to her custody by the end of March.

In late April, Piper successfully closed on her property. Her attorney managed to negotiate 75% of the funds be paid in advance. Piper took the money immediately and had found a modest four-bedroom house in Albany, Georgia.

The home was nothing compared to the mini mansion she lived in while married to Leland, but it had a fenced in yard and a pool for the kids to swim in. Most importantly it was at least one hundred miles away from Charles Brewer and that was just fine by Piper.

Pearl took a break from helping Piper pack and gazed out the front window. The rain shower had blown over and the kids were out front playing in the wet grass.

"It's a shame y'all have to leave." Pearl said sadly. "I was just getting used to having my grandbabies nearby."

Piper set a moving box down near the door. "Well...you know you're more than welcome to come with us, Mama. We have a spare bedroom just for you."

Pearl lowered her lids at Piper "Now you know damn well we can't live together."

"You're right." Piper giggled. "We would kill each other."

"Sure would" Pearl agreed chuckling. "I don't know what the hell Yance is thinking about moving all the way to Albany with your crazy butt."

Piper stuck out her tongue and Pearl continued. "Nah, I've been living in my house 39 years. I'm too old to be picking up moving anywhere. I'll leave that to you young people. Besides, I like Conners there are some mighty fine people here."

Hissing her teeth Piper wrapped her glass cups in newspaper. “I beg to differ. Only a handful of people I would call “Mighty Fine” and they don’t reside in this town. Especially the church folks.”

“To hell with the church folks.” Pearl snapped.

“They can all go straight to hell! I swear fore gawd, I ain't never stepping foot in that sanctuary again. I done found me a new church out in Mayville anyhow. And it ain’t Reverend Snowden’s church either. That bastard got the nerve to call my baby a Jezebel when he’s done laid up with every woman in his church.”

“Mama” Piper looked shocked. “How do you know that?”

“Everybody knows!” Pearl shrieked. “Half the women single in that church but they manage to keep popping out babies that just so happens to look like the Reverend every year. It ain’t immaculate conception!”

“Whew, chile, this is too much.” Piper shook her head at Pearl’s revelation.

A thought popped into Pearl’s head. “Speaking of Mayville, you never did tell me how your talk with that lady Margaret Robinson went.”

Piper sighed. “It went well. She gave me some information on a young lady who died on the army base where Charlie was a Sergeant. I got some detectives working on the case now.” “Good.” Pearl nodded. “Hopefully they can put that monster away soon.”

“Mrs. Robinson said her daughter Teresa felt like Charlie was watching her. I felt like he was watching me too. Teresa said Charlie seemed to know when she woke up in the morning and went to bed at night.”

Pearl’s brows furrowed “Well the only way he would know all that is if he was in the house with her.” A light bulb suddenly went off in Piper’s head, she stopped dead in her tracks and looked at her mother. “What if he was?”

Without waiting for a reply Piper took off down the hallway with Pearl right behind her. “What are we looking for?” Pearl asked once they made it to the master bathroom.

“I don’t know” Piper admitted as she looked around the room. “I’m not sure” Piper replied looking under the cabinets behind the mirror and inside the shower stall. “Just look for anything that looks out of place… anything that doesn’t belong.”

Pearl's brown eyes searched around the bathroom until she came across something that caught her eye. She pointed her finger "You mean like that?"

Piper followed Pearls direction to one of the electrical outlets on the wall. The plate was brand new but the screws holding it on the wall were stripped and tattered; like a Phillips head screwdriver had worn them down. Piper went to the kitchen to retrieve her toolbox and was back in a jiffy.

Once she unscrewed and saw the small marble sized disc behind the outlet her mouth fell open.

"Is that what I think it is?" Pearl asked.

"It's a camera." Piper confirmed suddenly overwhelmed with disgust knowing Charlie had probably seen her naked.

"We ought to look for more." Pearl demanded.

She and Piper searched every outlet and vent in the house. By the time they finished they had found five additional hidden cameras.

"That nasty, perverted bastard!" Piper gasped fighting back her tears.

"What are you going to do?" Pearl asked.

"I'm calling Yance!" Piper made a step towards her phone when she suddenly heard a child's terrified scream.

"Mama! Mama!" Phoebe shouted in a panic. Piper and Pearl rushed to the front door only to hear the haunting music…

Lights, Camera, Action. Have you singing, sorry Miss Jackson! Before she saw Charlie's truck parked on the front lawn. Piper couldn't believe the nerve of him let alone her eyes.

Charlie had gotten out of his truck and was dancing in Piper's front yard; stark naked and missing his eyeglasses. A half drunken bottle of Bird Dog liquor was clutched in one of his hands and a loaded pistol was clutched in the other. Charlie thrusted and gyrated his hips in a suggestive manner while his body jiggled to the beat.

"Lights, camera, actionnnnnnnn! I'm sorry Miss Jacksonnnnnnnnnn!" Charlie slurred.

"L.J. and Phoebe y'all come in the house. Mama call the police." Piper spoke calmly; never taking her eyes off Charlie.

The sudden movement of the children seemed to break Charlie from his trance. He stopped dancing and turned his attention on Piper now standing alone on the porch. There was a crazed look in his eyes; like a rabbit dog ready to bite.

"Oh, there you are, Darling." he grinned taking a swig from the bottle. "I hear you tryna' leave town. Now why you wanna go and do that for Baby?"

"Charlie get back in your truck and get the hell out of here." Piper demanded. "The police are on their way."

"The police?" Charlie chuckled. "Fuck the police! I own this town… I own you! Now come and give me some sugar, Gal." Charlie stumbled towards the porch.

Piper, suddenly remembering she still had the screwdriver in her hand. She jabbed it in the air. "Don't come any closer." She warned.

Charlie tried to focus his blurry eyes on the screwdriver. "Ah looka there. Miss Jackson got herself a weapon." He raised his gun and rubbed it along his exposed penis. "I got one too, Darling. But I would rather slay you with my mighty sword and this silver tongue I got."

Piper watched in horror as Charlie stuck out his tongue and began flickering it at Piper. "Oh, Baby that Pastor in Texas ain't got nothing on me. Come here gal!"

Before Piper knew it, she had stabbed at Charlie with the screwdriver. The tip of the tool left a gash over Charlie's right eye. He was so drunk he couldn't feel any pain. But he saw the blood gushing from his brow. He glared at Piper and raised his pistol.

"You bitch!"

Piper managed to run inside the house and lock the door before the bullets began to slice through the metal siding of the trailer.

"Get down!" She hollered at her children. She and Pearl dove on top of the kids as bullets whizzed past their head. Hearing the gunshots, Phoebe started to scream.

"Mama I'm scared!" L.J. cried underneath Piper. "Is Mr. Charlie going to kill us?"

"No Baby just keeps your head down." Piper answered.

"Lights camera actionnnnnnnnm! I'm sorry Miss Jacksonnnnnnnn! I'M SORRY MISS JACKSONNNNNNNN!" Charlie continued to scream like a mad man as he shot up the mobile home.

Suddenly police sirens could be heard in the distance. Piper was relieved to see flashing red and blue lights.

"Show me your hands, Mr. Brewer!" An officer shouted.

Piper rose up from her position on the floor and witnessed the police taking Charlie into custody. Deputy Williams pulled up in Piper's SUV and Piper ran out the door to meet him in the yard.

"What happened?" He asked confused as Piper sobbed uncontrollably in his arms. "You okay baby?"

Piper shook her head no just as Deputy Williams locked eyes with Charlie. A fit of anger washed over him. Storming up to Charlie he cold cocked Charlie so hard he fell flat on his ass bringing down two police officers with him.

"That's enough Yance!" Officer Tina warned. She was able to get Charlie in the back of the police cruiser and restore order. Watching the police drive off the property, Piper looked up at Yance.

"I'm so ready to say goodbye to that monster forever and start a new life the right way."

Deputy Williams smiled back. "I know me too."

Twenty-Six

"*D*eacon Brewer you have not only embarrassed yourself, but your sinful shenanigans have brought shame on us all." Deacon Brown paced back and forth inside the church's meeting room.

One hour after church elders had bailed Charlie out of jail he found himself in the church's meeting room surrounded by the angry members of the Deacon Board. The deacons had called an emergency meeting to discuss Charlie's unfortunate arrest. Charlie sat at the head of a long oak wood table with a dozen set of eyes glaring at him.

Deacon Brown quit pacing the floor momentarily to level a serious look on Charlie "Well Deacon do you have anything to say for yourself?" The other Deacons leaned in to hear Charlie's reply.

Charlie sucked in a small breath. "I'm sorry" he shrugged.

"You're sorry?" Deacon Brown grimaced in disgust. "What is sorry going to do for you when you're looking at spending the rest of your life in prison?"

“What?” Charlie chortled. “Don’t get carried away, Deacon. All’s I did was expose myself to the gal. Being a drunkard is hardly a reason for a life sentence, even in the state of Georgia. Piper Jackson set me up anyway. The whole town knows she’s been trying to get me to sleep with her. She asked me to come to her house. I finally gave in to her temptation and she got violent with me. Can’t you see, she’s the problem, not me. She’s a money hungry whore. I’m sure all we gotta do is throw a couple of dollars at her and she will drop the charges.”

The whole room fell silent. Charlie watched the other Deacons as they took turns offering each other awkward glances. It was Deacon Sims’ turn to speak. He eyed Charlie for a moment unsure if he wanted to tell him.

“Well Charlie” Deacon Sims finally spoke up. “I’m afraid it’s more complicated than you think. You see Miss Jackson done gone and found a lady out in Mayville say you killed her daughter.”

Charlie’s pace quickened. A ghost from his past had come back to haunt him. He tried to keep a straight face while beads of nervous sweat accumulated on his brow. “She’s a liar.”

“The lady done looked all into your past, Charlie. They got all kinds of dirt on you from back in your army days. Two investigators from Atlanta showed up here this morning asking about you. They looking into another young lady that was murdered and they saying you did it. Oh Charlie what have you done?"

"They're lying..." Charlie shook his head. "They're all lying. Deacon Sims, Deacon Brown, y'all know I wouldn't kill nobody. You know what kind of man I am. Like the *Good Book* says: *No weapon formed against me shall prosper.* In the end it will all work itself out I'm sure."

"You sure better hope so." Deacon Brown warned. "Because this entire town has put its reputation on the line for you. You better not let us down."

"I won't" Charlie assured them. "I won't, I swear."

On the outside Charlie appeared confident but as he watched his friends leave the room his heart pounded like he was threatening another heart attack. If his secrets got out his life and reputation would be ruined. Nobody could find out the truth about the murders. There was only one thing left for Charlie to do. He had to kill again.

###

The sun was setting by the time Margaret Robinson realized she had been out in her garden all day. In a year's time she had lost both her only child and her husband. One of the ladies at her church had suggested Margaret take up gardening as a way to cope with her loss. She had taken a liking to it immediately. Her favorite was bringing dead plants back to life. She'd wish she could do the same for her family.

Standing up to admire her rose bushes Margaret decided it was time to call it a night. She walked into the dimly lit house and removed her muddy gloves and straw hat. The local news was playing on the television; something about the governor and the upcoming elections. Margaret got herself cleaned up and stuck a Lean Cuisine in the microwave. She had cleared her spot to sit in front of the television and was just getting settled when the telephone rang.

"Hello?"

"Hello Mrs. Robinson, it's Piper how are you doing?"

"I'm making it" Margaret answered earnestly.

"How about yourself?"

“Oh, you don’t even want to know what I’ve been through this past week.” Piper let out a deep sigh. “Anyway I called to tell you that the investigation has officially started on Charles Brewer. I should be getting an update shortly. Hopefully we get justice for Teresa and any other victims of this sick monster.”

Margaret smiled. “I would appreciate that. Maybe my husband and baby girl will finally be able to Rest In Peace.”

“That’s what I’m hoping too. Oh yes the other reason why I called was to let you know that I have moved. I live in Albany now. I can give you my new address if you’d like.”

“Ok hold on let me place you on speaker phone while I find something to write with.” Margaret placed the phone down and began the task of rummaging through her cluttered drawers to find a pen.

Suddenly there was a loud thud. Margaret whipped her head in the direction of the back of the house. Making slow steps towards the sunroom Margaret craned her neck inside. About a year after the Robinson’s had purchased the house Earl Robinson had converted the patio into a beautiful sunroom for Margaret and Teresa to enjoy the sunny days and the starry nights. He would surely roll over in his grave if he saw the condition it was in now; packed to the brim with old furniture, half done art projects newspapers and magazines. Another loud thud erupted but Margaret dismissed the noise…Then she heard it again.

"Hello?"

"Yes, ma'am I'm still here" Piper replied through the speaker.

"Oh no not you. I thought someone was in my house." Margaret focused her eyes on the back of the house again. "Anyway, I have a pen what is your new address?"

Margaret wrote down the address and told Piper she would be in touch. She hung up the phone and proceeded to sit back down in front of the television. She ate her now lukewarm Lean Cuisine and was trying to focus on the television. One of her favorite crime shows was about to come on. ***BOOM!***

"Hello who's there?" Margaret called out into the darkness and got no answer. She sniffed the air. An overwhelming smell of gasoline and smoke crept up her nose.

Rising to her feet, Margaret followed the burning smell to the back of the house where there was also the sound of crackling. It was coming from the sun room. Margaret let out a gasp. The sunroom was on fire. She ran to the kitchen to get a bowl of water but it was too late. The old newspapers created the perfect ember. The entire sunroom was engulfed in flames in a matter of seconds.

She tried to escape through the laundry room, but it was on fire too. A thick blanket of black smoke blinded Margaret's vision. Her house was so hoarded with junk that she quickly got disoriented and couldn't find a way to escape the fire. She was being burned alive.

The fiery blaze warmed Charlie's face. He leaned up against his old truck with an empty metal gas can in his hand admiring his handy work. His tongue wet the toothpick he held in his mouth while he listened to Margaret Robinson scream like she was burning in the lake of fire.

Finally, satisfied that she was dead Charlie climbed into his truck. An evil smile crept onto his face. He had heard his beloved Piper on Margaret's speaker phone. He knew her address. The Good Lord was on his side and had sent him another sign that he and Piper were meant to be together. There was only one more obstacle that stood in Charlie's way and he was on his way to get rid of it.

"Soon my love… soon."

Twenty-Seven

Georgia Governor Frank Barrett is in legal trouble again after a video of him attempting to pay a prostitute for sex surfaced. Authorities say Governor Barrett used campaign funds to fuel his alleged extensive cocaine and sexual addiction. Barrett's legal team released a statement today saying their client denies these allegations and any wrongdoing. Further updates will be released to the public as this story unfolds. Back to you Jim.

Ruby Brewer sat in her lazy boy recliner fuming as the local news ran the clip of Governor Barrett's sex scandal for the sixth time in six hours. Usually Ruby enjoyed a good scandal but her mind was elsewhere.

"Where is he?" She peeked out the window. The church elders told Ruby that Charlie had been release from jail sometime after 9am that morning. Here it was after 11 o'clock at night and there was no sign of Charlie. The knuckle headed negro hadn't even bothered to call which pissed Ruby off even more. Every second that went by Ruby became more worried and she didn't like being worried. Being worried made her hungry and with no one there to feed her she got irritated.

Charlie had better have a good excuse for his disappearing act. The headlights on Charlie's truck lit up the living room as it finally pulled in the yard. Ruby primed her lips ready to give Charlie the tongue lashing of his life but when he didn't come right inside she was confused. She peeked out the window again.

Charlie was acting suspicious.
"What is this fool doing?" Ruby asked herself, watching Charlie scramble around the truck like his pants were on fire. He ran to the bed of his truck which was filled to the brim with plywood and pulled something out of the back.

"Charles!" Ruby screamed at the top of her lungs. "Charlie Brewer get your black ass in this house right now."

Charlie slammed the tailgate shut and calmly proceeded to the house with whatever object he retrieved from the truck tucked behind his back. When he entered the house he leaned up against the entrance of the living room and peered inside at Ruby. Ruby was slightly taken aback by Charlie's disheveled appearance. His glasses were missing, his hair was nappy, and it looked like he had not shaven in days.

"Where in the hell have you been?" Ruby

spoke in a low growl.

“I was with Deacon Sims.” Charlie spoke dryly.

“Liar!” Ruby yelled. “You must think I’m stupid. I know you wasn’t with no Deacon Sims. You don’t think I called the church, negro?”

Charlie shrugged. “Okay I lied. I wasn’t with Deacon Sims.”

Charlie’s nonchalant attitude was really grinding Ruby’s gears. She snarled at him. “I don’t know what the hell has gotten into you lately Charlie, but you’d better fix yourself before I go upside your head. You got five seconds to explain to me what you were doing with Pearls daughter at that trailer. Charlie I ain’t got time to play with you. After all these years of marriage you think you gone embarrass me you sorry sack of shit for brains? Let me tell you something right now...”

Charlie let out a yawn as Ruby began her favorite task; berating him. Her mouth was going a mile a minute as she proceeded to call him every foul belittling name she could think of.

“Charlie! Charlie are you listening to me? What is that you got behind your back?”

Charlie moved his hand to reveal the five-gallon metal gas can he had behind his back. Just then "BREAKING NEWS" flashed across the screen. *"Firefighters who rushed to put out a massive blaze in Mayberry, Georgia have discovered a body amongst the pile of rubble. The body is believed to be of 53-year-old Margaret Robinson. Foul play is suspected. More updates as this story unfolds."*

Ruby's hazel eyes peeled back with shock as she stared at Charlie. "Oh, my gawd Charlie, what did you do?"

The gas can crackled like thunder as it collided with Ruby's head. Her large body fell out of the lazy boy and crashed down onto the wood floor beneath her. She was seeing stars. The weight of her body was suffocating, making it difficult for her to breathe.

"You know Ruby after 39 years of marriage I think I'm just about sick of your mouth." He watched Ruby struggle to breathe.

The weight of her body cut off her air supply. She looked like a wounded manatee as she scooted across the floor. "Ruby there's something I've been meaning to tell you." Charlie casually reached in the front pocket of his coveralls, took out a tooth pick and placed it in his mouth. "Ya' see me and Piper... well we're together, Ruby. I know this news is hard for you to hear but, I love her and she loves me. We are meant to live together as husband and wife."

Ruby inched her way over to the edge of the settee an attempted to reach for the phone. The weight of Charlie's foot broke bones as it stepped on one of her hands. Ruby yelped in pain while Charlie ripped the phone cord out of its socket.

"I'm sorry to do this to you, Ruby. But she will give me a child. Something I always wanted. You can understand that can't you?"

Ruby continued to wail. "I know you're heartbroken over this Ruby." Charlie wrapped the cord around his hands and straddled Ruby like a hog. "We took a vow of till death do us part, I know. I don't believe in going back on the covenant I made with God. So, unfortunately Ruby this means yo' ass gotta go."

The cord cut into Ruby's flesh as it tightened like a noose around her neck. Charlie's face morphed into wild rage as he choked the life out of her. In an effort to try and save herself Ruby scratched Charlie's face infuriating him more. He choked her until the life finally left her eyes then stood up to catch his breath. Watching his wife of 39 years finally lying dead on the floor was a relief to Charlie. The old cow was finally put out of her misery. ***Fat! Funky! Bitch!***

Twenty-Eight

*I*t had been a week since Piper had left Conners and she was on a cloud. Adjusting to her new life in Albany felt like a dream. The city was easy to navigate. The neighbors in their small sub-division were all super friendly and welcoming. Yance, no longer the Deputy of Conners, was able to score an interview with the prestigious Albany Police Department right away.

Although Piper was nervous about uprooting the children once again and forcing them to get adjusted to yet another school system. She knew it had to be done in order to finally rid themselves of Charles Brewer.

It was getting late in the day on a Saturday in May and Piper was busy unpacking the last of the moving boxes. She was due to start her new position as Unit Clerk at Albany Medical Center on Monday and she wanted the home to be completely unpacked.

The keys started jingling in the door and Piper started to smile. Yance walked in without saying a word, wrapped his arms around Piper's waist and planted a kiss on her lips. Unable to read his demeanor Piper raised a brow

"Well?"

Yance let out a long-exasperated breath and his eyes fell to the floor. Suddenly a warm smile formed on his face when he looked up. "I got the job!" he shouted with glee.

"You did?" Piper cheered. "Oh, baby I knew you would get it!"

"You are looking at the newest member of the Albany Police Department. I'll be a beat cop for the time being, but the lieutenant liked me so much he wants me to apply for the Detective position that comes open in a few months. That position comes with a ten dollar raise and better benefits."

"I'm sure you will get that too." Piper kissed him passionately on the lips.

"So where are the kids?" Yance asked as they pulled away from their embrace.

"The next-door neighbor, Heather offered to take them with her kids to Chuckie Cheese and boy let me tell you, I couldn't get them outta here fast enough." Piper chuckled. "I got so much done today. I only have the kitchen left to unpack."

“Well here let me help you with that.” Yance offered.

“Ok umm... you can help me put up the fragile glass.” Piper said. She climbed on a step stool and added. “Just unwrap those glasses and hand them to me.”

“So, what do you think of the kid’s new school?” Yance handed her a glass to put away. “It’s cool right?”

“Oh man I am so excited for them.” Piper beamed. “They have a basketball team for LJ and an art program for Phoebe. I love both of their new teachers and most of the kids live in this neighborhood. I think we made a good move this time. Which is great because kids grow up so fast.”

“Maybe we should think about having another one soon, huh?”

Piper cut her eyes at Yance. “Another what?”

“Another kid!”

“Boy please” Piper guffawed. “First of all, I’m not even sure I want more kids but if I did want to have more, I would definitely need to be married first.”

"Cool, so when you want to get married?"

"I don't know-"

"How 'bout right now?"

Piper turned to see Yance on his knees; a ring in his hand and a serious look in his eyes.

"What are you doing?" Piper gasped in shock.

"Well I believe I'm asking you to be my wife."

Piper's eyes flickered with tears. "Are you sure?"

"I've never been more sure of anything in my life." Yance replied earnestly. "Piper, I have loved you since the first grade. I never stopped loving you even after I left to go to college. When I saw you again after all those years I knew I had to make you my wife. I know I agreed to take things slow but I'm a traditional country boy. You know we were not raised to shack up without being married. It just doesn't feel right living in sin. So what do you say, can we be a real family? Will you marry me? It's okay I even asked L.J. for permission."

Piper kneeled and planted a passionate kiss on Yance's lips. "Of course I will marry you."

"Hot damn!" Yance rose to his feet and place the ring on Piper's delicate finger "I can't wait to start calling you Mrs. Williams."

Piper giggled as he started planting sweet kisses all over her face and neck. Then the doorbell rang.

"Oh I'll get it." Piper chimed. "It's probably the neighbor lady back with the kids."

"Alright I'mma go take a shower." Yance said heading towards the bathroom.

Piper made her way to the front door and peeked through the peephole. The front porch was empty. She quickly unlocked the door thinking that maybe the package from Amazon she needed to hide from Yance was on the other side. There was no package on the other side of the door and Heather's green minivan was still missing from her driveway. Piper frowned as she looked around the yard. The sun was setting and not a soul was on the street. She shrugged and turned to walk back inside. That's when she was suddenly hit with 110 volts of electricity.

Inside the house Yance was preparing to take a shower. A sudden noise caught his attention. "Piper!" he called out but got no answer. He made it mid-way down the hallway when he realized the kids hadn't come stomping inside. “L.J.? Pheobe May? Piper!”

The front door was wide open and Piper was lying lifeless in the foyer.

“Oh my god! Piper!” Yance kneeled down beside her. “Piper wake up!”

Yance suddenly felt a jolt of electricity burn through his body. He never knew what hit him.

Twenty-Nine

*F*inally, Piper was all his and they could be together... Forever. Charlie giggled with excitement as Piper's lifeless body bounced around on the passenger side of his truck. She was beautiful even if she was unconscious. He imagined them as husband and wife coming back from a nice weekend stroll.

They had made it back onto Charlie's farm right as nightfall. He tossed Piper over his shoulder and carried her into the house. The house was dark and quiet as he proceeded cautiously towards the living room dropping Piper on the couch.

"Damn you heavy." Charlie huffed trying to catch his breath. He flipped on a light switch illuminating Pipers perfect brown face. Her eyes flickered open. She saw Charlie standing over her and bolted herself up right on the couch. Her doe eyes frantically scanned her surroundings. A wave of panic washed over her as she recognized the dimly lit living room.

"You're awake." Charlie beamed, his ashy lips spreading into a deranged smile "Welcome home, Darling."

Piper jumped up to her feet and bolted for the front door. Her heart sank once she realized there was no doorknob on the door; just a deadbolt that locked from the outside.

"Where do you think you're going Baby?" Charlie emerged from the living room. He was amused watching Piper's attempt to escape.

"Get away from me!" Piper shoved Charlie out of her way and made a mad dash for the kitchen to the back door; which was also locked from the outside. A sheet of plywood boarded up the screen.

"Shit!" Piper hissed as tears skated down her cheeks. "You can't escape, Darling." Charlie taunted her from the entrance of the kitchen. "All the windows and doors have been boarded up. You're not going anywhere. You belong to me now!"

"Let me out of here you sick bastard!" Piper screamed.

Charlie twisted his lips into a snarl. "Now is that any way to talk to your future husband? I know you're nervous, Piper. I am too. Why don't you come sit in the front room and let me fix you some dinner. We got us a big day ahead of us tomorrow. You and I are getting married!"

There was a door to Piper's left that hadn't

been boarded up. She was pretty sure the door lead to the cellar and that could possibly lead her to the outside.

"Get the hell away from me!" Piper screamed. She lifted a glass bowl full of apples from the kitchen counter and threw it at Charlie's head. The bowl hit the wall behind Charlie and shattered to the floor. The brief distraction gave Piper the chance to escape. She shot through the cellar door and stumbled down the stairs.

"No, Darling don't go down there." Charlie called out.

Piper ran down the steps so fast she ended up tripping on the last step and falling forward. She landed head first on what she thought was a pile of clothes. But, then she felt hair; and a human's hand. When Piper realized she was staring face to face with the dead corpse of Ruby Brewer she let out an earth shattering scream. She scrambled to get away just as Charlie stood over her with a metal bat in his hand.

"No! Please! Mr. Charlie no!"

Charlie raised the bat high in the air and brought it down over Piper's head with the force of thunder. She was knocked out cold.

###

A loud ringing noise echoed inside Yance's ear. It took him a moment to realize the noise was coming from the other side of the doorbell and not from the massive migraine inside his head. He slowly rose to his feet feeling disoriented and groggy. The doorbell rang again.

"Coming" he called. He walked to the door with his head feeling like it had been through an ax grinder. He felt wetness on the back of his head. It was blood. *What the hell happened?*

He opened the door to the kids and his next-door neighbor Heather standing on the other side with her arms folded. "I was about to call the police." she spat with an attitude. "I've been trying to get in touch with y'all since yesterday."

"Yesterday?" Yance asked confused; The headache he was experiencing made it worse by the blinding sunlight. "W-What's today?"

"Today is Sunday and I have three kids to get ready for church. If Piper wanted me to keep the kids past a couple of hours, then she should've-"

"Piper? Oh my God where's Piper?" Yance's eyes peeled back in horror as the previous day events played out in his mind. Piper was gone. Someone had taken her. But who? Yance had an idea.

“Where’s mama?” L.J. asked looking around.

Yance looked at Heather. “I’m so sorry do you mind watching the kids. I need to go.”

“Is everything alright?”

“No!” Yance had grabbed his keys and was in his car before Heather could say another word. He hopped in the car and whipped out his cell phone.

One hundred miles away Conners newest Deputy Hank Brown was at his desk with his feet propped. His Stetson covered his face as he snored softly. Nearby Officer Tina Adams was watching the latest episode of Jerry Springer on a thirteen inch portable television. It was another lazy day in Conners with nothing to do. Then suddenly the phone rang.

Tina reached for the phone with her eyes still glued to the television screen.
“Conners Police Department. Officer Adams speaking-”

“Tina! It’s Yance I need your help!” Yance blurted out in one breath.

“Yance?” Tina looked confused.

“What seems to be the problem?”

“It’s Piper”

“What happened now?”

“She’s been kidnapped. I believe Charles Brewer has her.”

Tina rolled her eyes heavenward “Did you see Mr. Brewer take Piper?”

“Well no but-”

“Then how do you know it was him?”

“Because I know!” Yance shouted through the receiver. “Listen Piper is missing. She was kidnapped and I just know he has her. I’m an hour and a half away. Please just go over there and you will see.”

“Okay.” Tina let out a yawn. “We will go check. But without proof there isn’t much we can do.”

“Thank you, Tina.” Yance said disconnecting the call.

Officer Tina placed the phone down on the receiver and continued to watch her television program.

“Who was that?” Officer Hank asked.

“Just Yance.” Officer Tina said nonchalantly. “He thinks Charlie Brewer has kidnapped his girlfriend. Wants me to go over to the Brewer farm to have a look.”

“You want me to go?”

“No, I’ll go.” Officer Tina replied. “Just as soon as my show goes off.”

Thirty

When Piper awoke it was morning. She was wearing a thin piece of pink lingerie; naked underneath. Laying on her back in an old four poster bed. A clock on the wall ticked just loud enough to make her head pound. She went to sit up but something was wrong. She couldn't move her arms or legs. She couldn't wiggle her fingers or toes. She couldn't move her head either. Her whole body felt numb. Panic began to set in once Piper realized she was now paralyzed.

"Oh My Love you're awake." Charlie entered the outdated bedroom carrying a tray of breakfast foods.

"Now I know you like your eggs scrambled with cheese but I forgot how you like your bacon fried. I hope you like it fried hard."

Tears that she was unable to wipe away welled up in Piper's eyes as she watched Charlie place the tray down beside her.

"Oh, Darling you must be so happy, you're crying tears of joy." Charlie wiped away her tears and propped her head up on a pillow. He then took a fork and scooped up a mound of eggs. “Alright now open up, Darling.”

The food was scorching hot to Piper’s lips but she was unable to scream. She could only moan in agony.

“I said open your mouth, Piper.” Charlie’s eyes flashed with anger as he became agitated. “I went through all this trouble to make you a nice breakfast and I won’t have you be ungrateful. Ya’ hear me? Now open your damn mouth, Bitch!”

Piper continued to moan in fear as Charlie stabbed her lips with the forkful of food. Then suddenly as his manic episode came, it dawned on Charlie that Piper was unable to move and he began to laugh hysterically. He placed the fork back on the tray.

“I forgot you can’t open your mouth can you, Darling.” He reached over and moved a wisp of hair from Piper’s eyes. “That’s because I gave you a little bit of tranquilizer. I gives it to my pigs sometimes when I need to keep them calm. I thought it would’ve been out of your system by now.”

Charlie wrinkled his forehead then shrugged “Oh well we can eat later I suppose.” His eyes instantly filled with lust as he eyed Piper’s naked body thinly veiled in the pink lace lingerie he picked out for her. He had imagined how her body would look in it for months, but nothing could compare to the vision of beauty before him.

"Gosh you're beautiful." He shook his head. "Umph, umph, humph… I can't wait to marry you today. You don't mind if I sample these goods do you? Of course, you don't"

Piper began to sob as Charlie's rough hands groped and felt up on her body. He slipped the straps from her shoulders exposing her nipples to the cool air.

"Ooh look at ya' getting excited." Charlie smiled before suckling one of her breast. She cringed and squirmed in agony as his cold slimy tongue circled her nipple. He roughly pinched and yanked on her other nipple with his free hand. His dirty nails dug into her supple flesh. He brought his large ashy lips to hers and attempted to kiss her. His breath smelled of liquor and bile as he stabbed his tongue down her throat.

If hell was a real place Piper was sure she was living in it as the Devil himself continued to violate her body. Just when Piper was sure it couldn't get any worse she heard the jingling of Charlie's belt buckle. She tensed up and looked on with shock as he undid his trousers.

Oh my God is he... Is he going to rape me? Please

God! Please God no! Piper silently prayed. She willed herself to get up; to fight. But it was no use she couldn't move.

Straddling her body at the waist Charlie began to moan with pleasure as he stroked his erect penis.

"Ugh Oh God....Ssssss....SHIT"

Charlie let a howl as he climaxed, ejaculating sperm all over Piper's exposed breast and chin. She pinched her lips together best she could to keep the salty liquid from seeping into her mouth.

Oh God please let this be over soon.

"Oops looks like I made a mess." Charlie covered his mouth with his hand and chuckled "I cannot wait to make you my wife and make love to you every single day. I'll be back with a hot wash rag to clean you up."

Charlie disappeared out of the bedroom. Tears continued to flow. Piper realized she might be trapped in this house with a mad man for the rest of her life. She remembered watching the story of the three young girls held captive by an evil man in Ohio for ten years. Ten years before they were found. Ten Years! Her babies would be grown. She would have missed out on raising them. All because she had accepted the help of a Good Deacon. Pearl tried to warn her.

Oh mama why didn't I listen to you? Piper cried "Why!"

Piper startled herself when she heard the word come out of her mouth. She could speak! Could she move? Piper wiggled her fingers; then moved her arms. Her legs still felt like a ton of bricks had been laid on top of them and she was unable to move the bottom half of her body. But the top half still work and that was she needed to give her hope.

"Darling I thought I heard you in here talking." Charlie returned with a steamy hot wash cloth.

Piper quickly regressed back to her feeble position. She couldn't let him know she was half mobile. He wiped his semen off her body and slid the straps back up her shoulders. Just as he was about to try and fondle her again the doorbell rang.

Charlie looked to Piper with a confused expression etched on his face. "Well I wasn't expecting company" he said "Be right back. Don't you go no where."

Thank you, Jesus! Piper let out a sigh of relief.

Charlie made his way down the hallway and scanned his surroundings before opening the door. He was shocked to see the police on the other side of the door.

"Morning Charlie how are you on this fine Sunday morning?" Officer Tina asked with a smile.

"Oh, I'm making it." Charlie replied. "What brings you by?"

"I really hate to bother you, but I have to follow up on a complaint." Officer Tina said.

Charlie's forehead wrinkled. "Complaint?"

"Piper Jackson has gone missing. Yance Williams seems to think you may know something about her disappearance."

"I don't know why he would think that." Charlie let out a nervous chuckle "I haven't seen either one of them since they left town."

"I figured that." Officer Tina nodded "Sorry to waste your time Mr. Charlie."

"No problem Darling" Charlie started to close the door

"Wait!" Officer Tina shouted. "While I'm here let me say hi to Mrs. Ruby."

Charlie resisted the urge to roll his eyes. "You can't. I'm sorry, but Ruby is not here."

"Oh."

"Yeah, she left yesterday to go visit her sister up in Rochester, New York." Charlie lied quickly. "Nobody in here but me until she returns. Alright bye-bye now."

BOOM! "Help! Somebody help me!" Piper shouted.

Officer Tina's eyes widened in shock. She and Charlie locked eyes before she went for her weapon. They wrestled for Officer Tina's revolver out on the porch then inside the house.

Meanwhile the affects of the tranquilizer was starting to wear off. Piper, still unable to move her legs, crawled on her elbows. Tears fell from her eyes as she struggled against the hardwood floor. She made it out into the hallway. Charlie was fighting with the police officer. They were now tussling on the ground fighting for the weapon.

If only Piper could make it over to them, she could help the officer. She inched closer… then closer. She was almost there then… ***POW!***

All hopc Piper had of escaping was lost as she watched Charlie straddle over Officer Tina with a smoking gun aimed at her head. With his chest heaving and his glasses knocked off his face Charlie looked up and locked eyes with Piper.

"You!" He rose to his feet in a fit of anger. "You see what you made me do! You are a stupid bitch! I wasn't gonna kill nobody else and now I done killed the police! Look what you made me do!"

Charlie tucked the pistol in his waistband, stomped over to Piper and grabbed her by the hair.

Piper screamed in agony as he drug her down the hallway towards the back door then across the yard into his pole barn.

"Stupid bitch!" Charlie spat tossing Piper headfirst in a pile of hay.

The smell of pig feces filled her nose. Piper frantically scanned her surroundings. Dozens of candles lined a makeshift altar made of wood.

"Welcome to your wedding day." Charlie said defeated. "I planned a real beautiful thing for us Piper but now your dumbass had to gone and ruin it. Now we have to get married in a rush so that we can be together."

Charlie walked over to a rusty trunk and pulled out an old wedding dress. The dress was crumpled, rotted, and fraying at the sleeves. "This used to be Ruby's. It'll probably fit a little big on you but it will still get the job done." Charlie tossed the dress at Piper and demanded. "Put it on."

Slowly Piper stood up on her wobbly legs. The affects of the tranquilizer still left her legs extremely numb and tingly. Not wanting to anger Charlie further, Piper took off the lingerie and slipped Ruby's wedding dress over her naked body. The lace was itchy, and the shoulder pads slipped off her shoulders in the ill-fitting dress.

"Well aren't you just a vision to behold." Charlie smiled with glee. He placed the veil over her head. "Let's get married, Darling."

He forced her to the makeshift alter. There were so many candles they were blinding. A fire slowly burned in a barrel. The heat caused Piper to sweat under the heavy material of the wedding gown. Charlie reached inside the trunk and pulled out a long black robe; one that would be worn by a priest or Baptist preacher. He took Officer Tina's gun and laid it down on the altar.

"It's time to say our vows, Darling. I know you haven't had a chance to come up with yours yet so I wrote them for you."

Charlie reached in the front pocket of the robe and pulled out a folded sheet of paper.

"Here you read this." He shoved the paper into Piper's hand. When she failed to start reading he took the pistol and pointed it at her head "I said read it."

With tears skating down her cheeks Piper read the vows aloud with her hand trembling.

"I-I... Piper... take you Charlie... to be my...h-husband. I will be a good wife. A dutiful wife. I will cater to all your needs. I will be obedient. I will not be selfish. I will not get fat and I will keep the house clean. I will also give you your own first born s-son. I will be your wife in life and in...d-death."

Piper sobbed uncontrollably "Mr. Charlie please-"

"Okay now my turn." Charlie sat the gun down, unfolded his paper and cleared his throat "Okay Miss

Piper I graciously take you to be my wife. I will feed you. I will make sweet love to you everyday and every night. I will love you with all of my heart and I will only beat your ass when you make me mad."

He looked up at Piper and flashed a deranged smile "But I don't think I'll have to put my hands on you much. I mean once you learn your place and all."

He forced Piper to lock her hands with his.

"Now usually people swap rings at this time. But I thought for our love we needed something a little bit more permanent."

Piper's face etched with confusion as Charlie pulled her over to the fire pit. She looked on with horror as she watched Charlie reach into the fire and pull out a metal wire in the shape of ring. The end of it burned a fire orange.

"Wait" Piper panicked "Wait what are you doing."

"This'll only hurt for a second, Darling."

"Wait! Charlie no!"

Thirty-One

Yance did a hundred down the highway. His adrenaline was pumping so hard he didn't notice his head injury. Merging off the next exit he made a B-line for the Brewer farm. Yance parked on the side of the dirt road leaving the car running and ran the rest of the way to Charlie's property with his gun in his hand.

Spotting the police car in the yard, he cautiously made his way up to the front door. Noticing the windows were all boarded up Yance proceeded onto the porch. A small boot was sticking out the front door alerting him of danger.

Yance tip toed up the steps and slowly opened the door. Officer Tina was lying lifeless in the foyer.

"Jesus Christ!" Yance rushed to Officer Tina's side and pulled her radio. "Officer down!" He shouted into the receiver. "I repeat officer down! Get a crew out to the Brewer farm right now. I haven't located the suspect but he is armed and dangerous so take caution."

Yance tossed the radio and stood to his feet raising his gun. Bracing himself he made his way throughout the Brewer home. Nothing seemed out of place. The house was dimly lit and eery. There was no sign of Piper yet he knew she was there somewhere. Yance could feel her presence and smell her scent.

The door to the cellar was ajar. He slowly made his way to it and peered inside. Hitting the light switch, he gasped at the sight of Ruby Brewer laying at the bottom of the steps. Suddenly Yance heard Piper's blood curdling scream coming from the back of the house and headed that way.

Outside the back door Yance saw the pole barn. He could see movement coming from inside. As he got closer he could see inside. Candles. An altar. As soft classical music played. The hairs on the back of Yance's neck prickled when he noticed Piper in a wedding dress. She was weeping and nursing a burn on her left hand; her ring finger.

"I now pronounce us husband and wife!" Charlie smiled. He gazed lovingly at the burn on Piper's ring finger. He had branded her. She would be his forever. "Now come and kiss your husband." Charlie tried to plant a kiss on Piper as she turned away.

"Please Mr. Charlie..." she sobbed. "Please you gotta let me go."

"Nah, Darling. I'm afraid I can't let you do that."

"But I have a life with family and friends."

"I'm your family now. You don't need no friends. All you need is me."

"But what about my kids?"

"Fuck them badass kids!" Charlie backhanded Piper causing her to fly backwards into the pile of hay.

"See what you made me do!" Charlie rushed to help Piper off the ground.

"Get off of me you sick bastard!" Piper yanked her arm from his grasp.

"You shouldn't be upset on your wedding day. It just ain't right." Charlie thought for a second. "I know what will make you happy… I'll play our song." He walked over to the small rickety stereo.

Piper grimaced when the familiar music started to play. ***Uh shorty, turn it around lemme see somethin'/ Messing with me for real, it's gone be somethin'/ Yea, I'm talking Lights, Camera, Action/ Had me singin', I'm sorry Miss Jackson!***

"Come on Darling, we gotta celebrate!" Charlie yelled over the music. "Lets dance." He yanked Piper close to him and forced her to dance with him. Just as she was about to give up, she saw the face of God looking back at her.

It was Yance and he was creeping up behind Charlie. Instinctively Piper wrapped her arms around Charlie and began to dance on him.

"I love you Piper" Charlie whispered into her ear licking her earlobe.

Piper shivered at the feel of his saliva; nearly vomiting as Charlie held her close, gyrating against her thigh.

"I've been waiting for this moment since the day I laid eyes on you." Charlie whispered softly in her ear.

WHAP! Yance hit Charlie so hard with his pistol he fell to the ground. "Argh!" Charlie grimaced as blood leaked down his shirt. That still wasn't enough to keep a monster like Charles Brewer down.

Piper's eyes suddenly flashed with terror. "Yance look out!"

Yance spun around just in time as Charlie charged him. His gun flew from his grasp and landed in the hay. He landed a punch to Charlie's gut then another one. Nothing was stopping Charlie as he charged full force at Yance again. The weight of his body sent both men flying over the altar. A tiny candle tipped over and an ember ignited. The dried hay caught fire quickly and before long the whole barn was on fire.

Piglets began to squeal as the fire got closer to their 8 by 16 foot pens. Piper screamed as the two men engaged in an epic battle; both men fighting with all their might for the love of Piper.

Mustering up his balance Mr. Charlie lunged for Yance landing a right jab, then a left. The two of them squared off tussling around in the hay. Mr. Charlie laughed sinisterly as he got the best of Yance.

"You's a weak boy!" Charles Brewer taunted standing over Yance.

Yance tripped Charlie; landing haymaker after haymaker causing Charlie to fall backwards. His face was covered in blood. One of his eyes was swollen shut. Clutching his chest and feeling the jerking pain of another heart attack Charlie clutched his chest and gathered his breath. Down by his ankles he saw Officer Tina's gun. Yance saw it too. The two men made a mad dash for the weapon but Piper got to it first. She aimed the gun at Charlie's head.

"Don't fucking move!" Piper warned him; coughing from smoke inhalation.

Both men froze. The fire danced off the bundles of hay itching it's way near them. Sirens wailed nearby. Piper continued to take aim as the smoke burned her eyes.

The corner of Charlie's lips curled in a sinister smile.

"Now whatchu gone do with that big ol thang, Darling?" He asked inching closer "Give me the gun Darling you wouldn't-"

BOOM! Piper squeezed the trigger; her hands shaking.

"Shhh, it's okay Baby. Hand me the gun." Yance removed the pistol out of Piper's hand. She looked up at Yance with her chest heaving.

"I love you." She cried hysterically.

"I love you too Baby." Yance grabbed Piper up in his arms and lead her out of the pole barn just as police cruisers descended onto the Brewer farm . "I promise you this animal will never hurt you again."

Epilogue

9 months later…

Yance stood at the doorway of the nursery looking at the tiny feet kicking inside the crib. A room painted in blush pink and mint green with large white elephants painted on the wall provided the perfect décor for his baby girl's nursery.

"You know you don't have to stare at her every second." Piper walked up and hugged him from behind. "She's perfectly fine entertaining herself until she falls asleep."

"I know... I just can't believe how beautiful she is." Yance smiled. "You know she gets her good looks from me." Piper rolled her eyes heavenward.

"Whatever, I'd better get dinner started. The kids will be home from school in a minute." Piper made her way down the hallway then stopped. "Did you check the mail like I asked?"

"I sure did Mrs. Williams" Yance smiled lovingly at her. "It's on the kitchen counter waiting on you to go through it, Beautiful."

Piper couldn't hide the smile as she made her way to the kitchen to start dinner. She had been through a lot in such a short time. Finally, her life was what she always imagined it would be. She had her charming husband, her beautiful kids, a supportive church family, a steady job, and a house on the hill. For once all was normal and Piper was extremely happy.

Charles Brewer was convicted of four murders and the attempted murder of Officer Tina Adams and was sentenced to serve four life terms in the Georgia State Penitentiary.

Piper had gone on to marry Yance Williams in a small ceremony surrounded by close family and friends. Yance completed the paperwork to adopt Piper's children. The kids were excited to hold the "Williams" last name especially Phoebe May who claimed she knew all along that Yance Williams would be her step-daddy.

Shortly after making the announcement that she and Yance were expecting a child, Jamie Lynn and Josh informed them that they too were expecting baby number ten. Jamie Lynn was happy as a clam and was already planning a double baby shower and play dates.

Pearl was on cloud nine after Piper gave birth to her third grandchild and insisted on naming her. After constant back and forth they all decided on the name Yasmin Renee Williams. Still on maternity leave Piper was trying to get her body geared up to go back to work in just a few weeks.

Removing a pack of frozen chicken from the freezer Piper placed it in the sink. Turning the faucet on to lukewarm, she allowed the meat to thaw while she sat at the counter and began the task of sorting through the mail. Nothing out of the ordinary except for the typical bills, the local grocery store circular, and a coupon for a free oil change.

Gathering up the junk mail for the trash something else caught Piper's eye. It was an envelope from the Georgia State Penitentiary addressed to her.

Piper's hand trembled as she saw the sender's name on the top left-hand corner. C-H-A-R-L-E-S B-R-E-W-E-R was written out in bold neat letters. The hairs on the back of her neck prickled.

How on God's green earth did he find her from prison? The attorney had assured her Mr. Charlie would never be able to contact her again. Piper's heart sank in her chest as she wrestled with the thought of opening the letter. Then curiosity got the best of her as she finally decided to open it.

Dear Piper Brewer,

How are you my sweet Darling? All is well with you, I hope. I'm doing fine for an old man. This place reminds me of my army days. They give me three hots and a cot and gave me a job as the Chaplin in the church. My lawyer says that I will be here for the rest of my life, but I know in my heart that it is not in God's plan. So I will be out of here soon and when I do we can finish the love story that we started. I know that you are missing me but please be patient. We will be reunited soon… Until then please accept the gift I have left you with. I believe you call her Yasmin. I hope she has your eyes and my smile. I'm not too fond of the girls so we will have to make us a boy too when I get out of here. I know what you're thinking I can assure you that you enjoyed every second of our union even though you were unconscious. Don't worry our baby is not a bastard that is why I made sure that we are married in the eyes of God. I won't leave you to raise this baby on your own I promise. I'm sorry if I hurt you and I plan to spend the rest of our lives making it up to you.

Until then Darling

Lights! Camera! Action!

Thanks, I hope you enjoyed!!!

I am always eager to connect with new readers. Please follow me on any one of my social media platforms

Facebook: Autumn Crum
and
Crum Publishing LLC
Instagram: Author_Autumn_Crum

Twitter: @AutumnDaAuthor

Goodreads: Autumn Crum

Search: #AutumnCrum

Made in the USA
Columbia, SC
20 December 2022